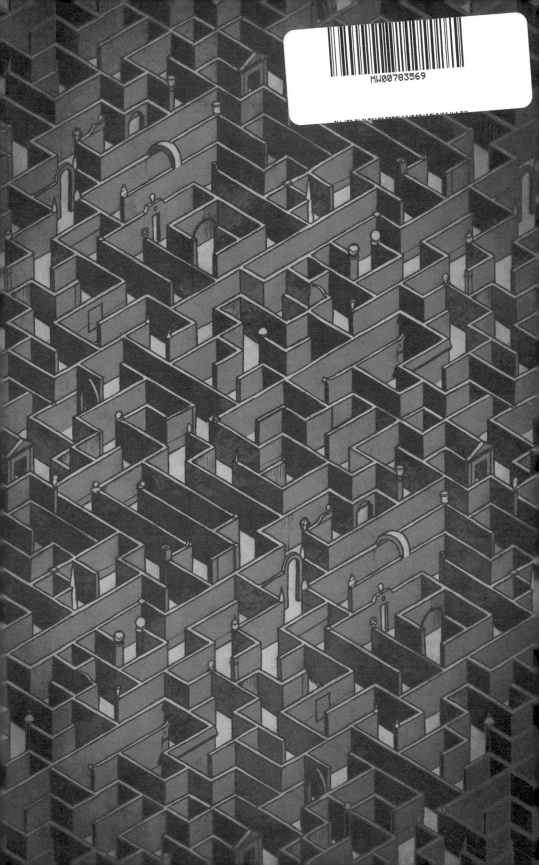

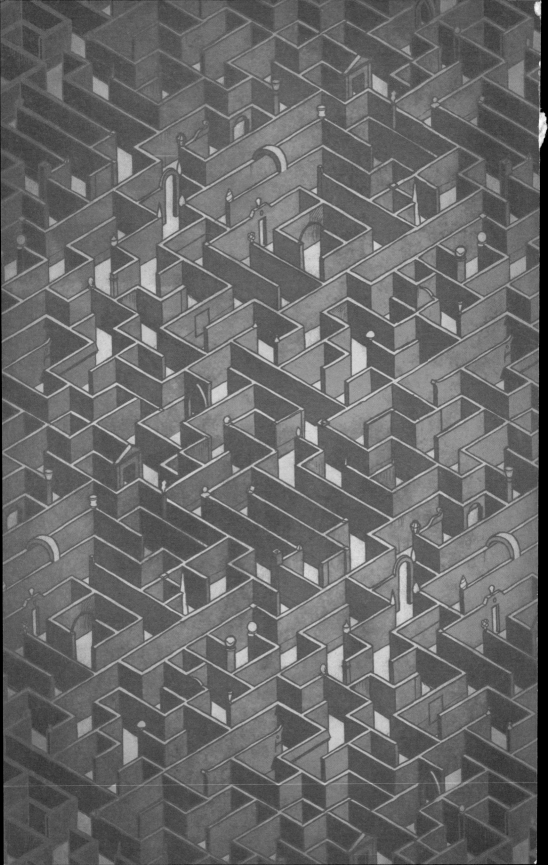

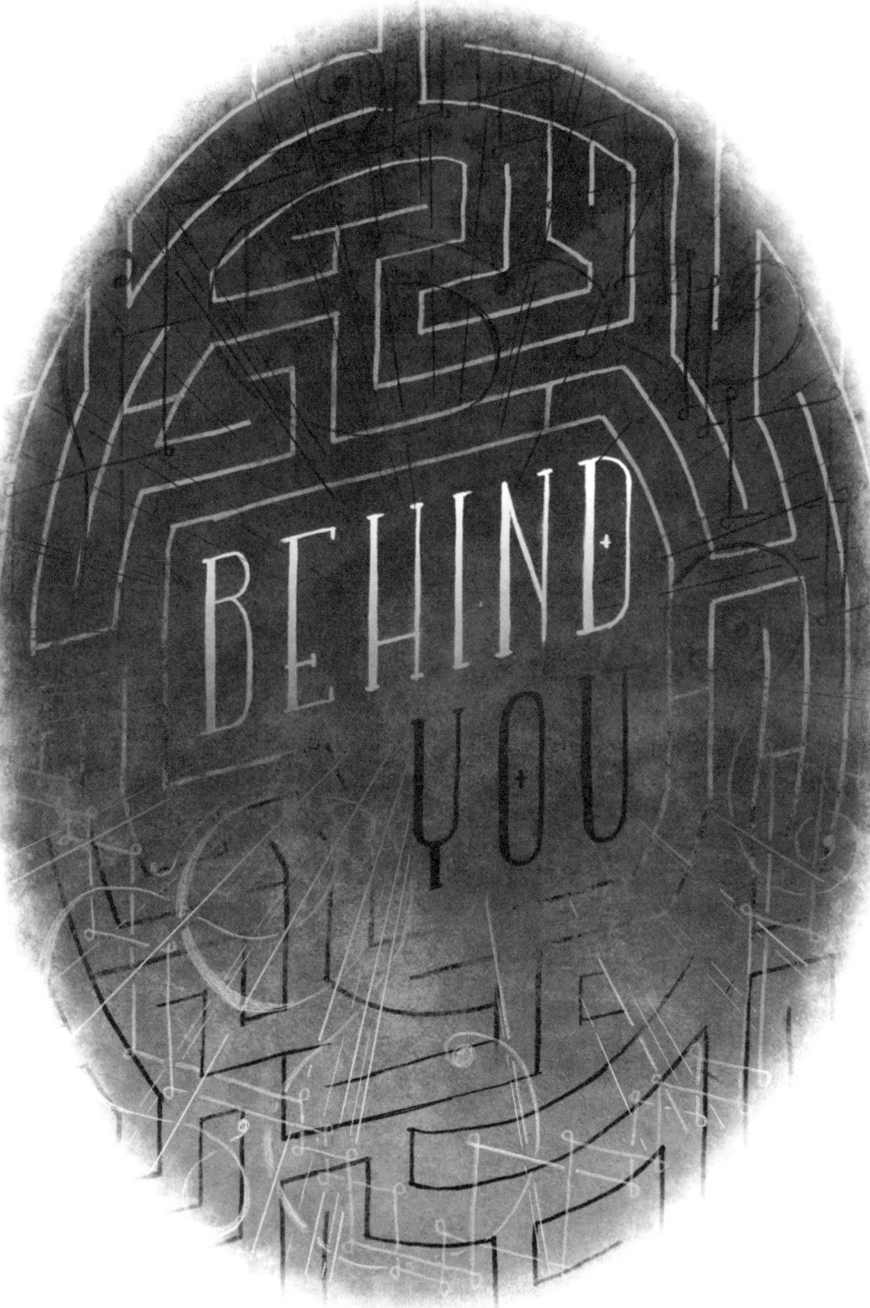
BEHIND
YOU

www.idwpublishing.com

ISBN: 978-1-63140-953-0

20 19 18 17   1 2 3 4

Collection Edited by Justin Eisinger and Alonzo Simon
Production by Gilberto Lazcano
Publisher: Ted Adams

For international rights, contact licensing@idwpublishing.com

Ted Adams, CEO & Publisher • Greg Goldstein, President & COO • Robbie Robbins, EVP/Sr. Graphic Artist • Chris Ryall, Chief Creative Officer • David Hedgecock, Editor-in-Chief • Laurie Windrow, Senior Vice President of Sales & Marketing • Matthew Ruzicka, CPA, Chief Financial Officer • Lorelei Bunjes, VP of Digital Services • Jerry Bennington, VP of New Product Development

Facebook: facebook.com/idwpublishing • Twitter: @idwpublishing • YouTube: youtube.com/idwpublishing
Tumblr: tumblr.idwpublishing.com • Instagram: instagram.com/idwpublishing

for
Kate

When You Are Alone
You Are Never Alone
by
Joe Hill

1.

Lots of old houses in New England contain odd little doors in odd little corners. These are doors too small for adults – only a child could crawl through them, into the darkness on the other side, where the walls are bare lathing, and the floor is sometimes dirt. My Great-Aunt Ethelyn told me Mister Alamagüselim lives behind all such little doors and that children who go away with him never come back.

To this day, if I notice an Alamagüselim door, I cannot sit down with my back to it.

2.

Brian Coldrick has a blog called Behind You (thehairsonthebackofyourneck.tumblr.com) showcasing his single panel comics: images of lonely people in lonely places thinking lonely thoughts.

Only the comics are *alive*.

That is, they are lightly animated. Candleflames flicker. Rain trickles down the windows. Shadows waver and bob.

And there is always something moving in the darkness behind his lead characters, something they haven't seen yet. Something we are afraid they won't see until it's too late for them.

It is the simplest of conceits and it should grow old quickly and it never does. Every image produces a fresh prickle of alarm and dread. Brian has, I think, distilled an entire genre of fiction to its most fundamental form. He has refined and purified the entire idea of Horror to a single, vital idea: you need to keep looking behind you because you never know when you might catch something creeping up on you. Something skinless with a glistening mouth full of fangs, leaving red footprints. Something shivering and cold and eager to button on a new coat of flesh. Your flesh.

Mathias Clasen, a Danish literary theorist who applies the findings of evolutionary biology to our understanding of genre, has argued persuasively that our affection for horror fiction is a survival mechanism. We use our imaginations to project ourselves into scenarios of threat and predation. It's useful. No one wants to be hunted for real. But in a fictional setting, we can experience all the panic and dizzying suspense of the hunt, without any of the risk, and in this way prepare, perhaps, for the potential of the real thing. Because, of course, even now, here in the modern world of high-speed internet and self-driving cars, there are things out there pretending to be human that would be happy to wear your skin. And we all need to be ready for them.

So, you see: Brian Coldrick is performing a public service by scaring you sick.

3.

The illustrations in this book aren't animated, because they're printed on paper.

Nothing in the pictures will suddenly move any closer to Brian Coldrick's hapless, clueless heroes. None of the creatures will look around and notice *you*. You're safe.

So go ahead and read them at night, when you're alone, by candleflame. You'll be fine. I promise.

4

Each of Brian's illustrations comes with one or two lines of text – sometimes not even an entire sentence, just a fragment of a thought – hinting at much larger stories, whole novels maybe. They're a little like *New Yorker* cartoons, if David Cronenberg or Peter Straub did *New Yorker* cartoons. A few of them are even funny, in a dry, morbid sort of way.

Which reminds me of a thing I learned a while back. A doctor told me that sometimes, when a person gets a leg blown off, and they see the stump below their knee, they'll laugh before they scream. Apparently the visual is so startling and surreal it just naturally produces a little cry of hilarity.

It's so funny to discover you're made of meat and at any moment the world might take a bite. Our species comes wired with a great sense of humor. It's one of our best traits.

5

You can absorb all the horror of a Brian Coldrick illustration in a single glance, but you can *live* with any of his pictures for much longer, building out the implied story in your mind. For example: in this book you will discover an illustration of a girl assembling a puzzle, while a hideous phantom is assembled behind her, materializing out of thin air, one stringy artery and one filthy bone at a time "She loved puzzles. She couldn't resist them. Piece by piece it revealed itself."

I want to know everything that came before the moment in the illustration, and everything that will come after. In my own version of the story, she turns and discovers the deformity behind her, and sensibly dashes the puzzle to the floor, shattering him in an instant. But later... later, she rebuilds him, and offers to let him live, if he'll deal with the other girls in the neighborhood, the ones who are so mean to her. She'll even pull one of the other puzzles down off the shelf and construct him a friend.

Brian's suggestive words are, in their own way, as thrilling as his suggestive art. The pictures inspire shock, while his sentences invite you to linger, to make yourself at home, to dream bad dreams.

Suspense is the force that drives you to turn the page, and find out what happens next, in hope of discovering some relief, some comfort, some easing of your horror.

But Brian offers you no relief and no comfort. Turn the page, and you only find a fragment of another story. He will never tell you what happens next to any of his menaced protagonists. You have to imagine the rest of each tale for yourself.

If there is a way out for any of his heroes, you will have to be the one to find it.

6.

Each of these illustrations is a little door into a little world. On the other side of that door is Mister Alamagüselim and things far worse than Mister Alamagüselim.

Open the first and climb in. The way is shadowy and the ceiling is low. You may have to crawl. The air is stale. The floor is filthy. No matter what, keep going.

I know it's scary to be all alone in the dark. But not as frightening as when you realize you aren't.

Joe Hill
New Rochelle,
NY
24 June, 2017

always behind you

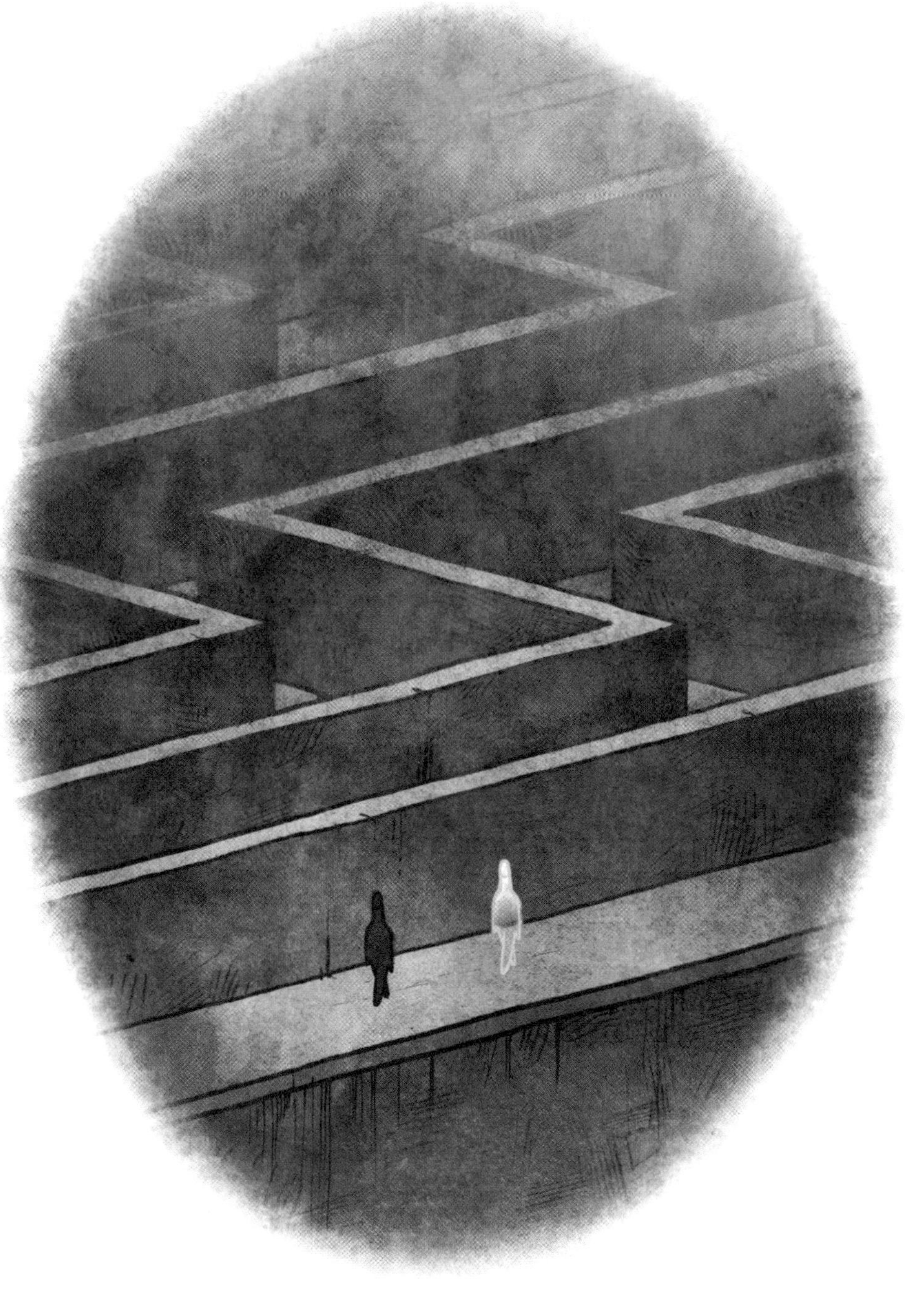

on the way back to bed, he heard the floorboards creak

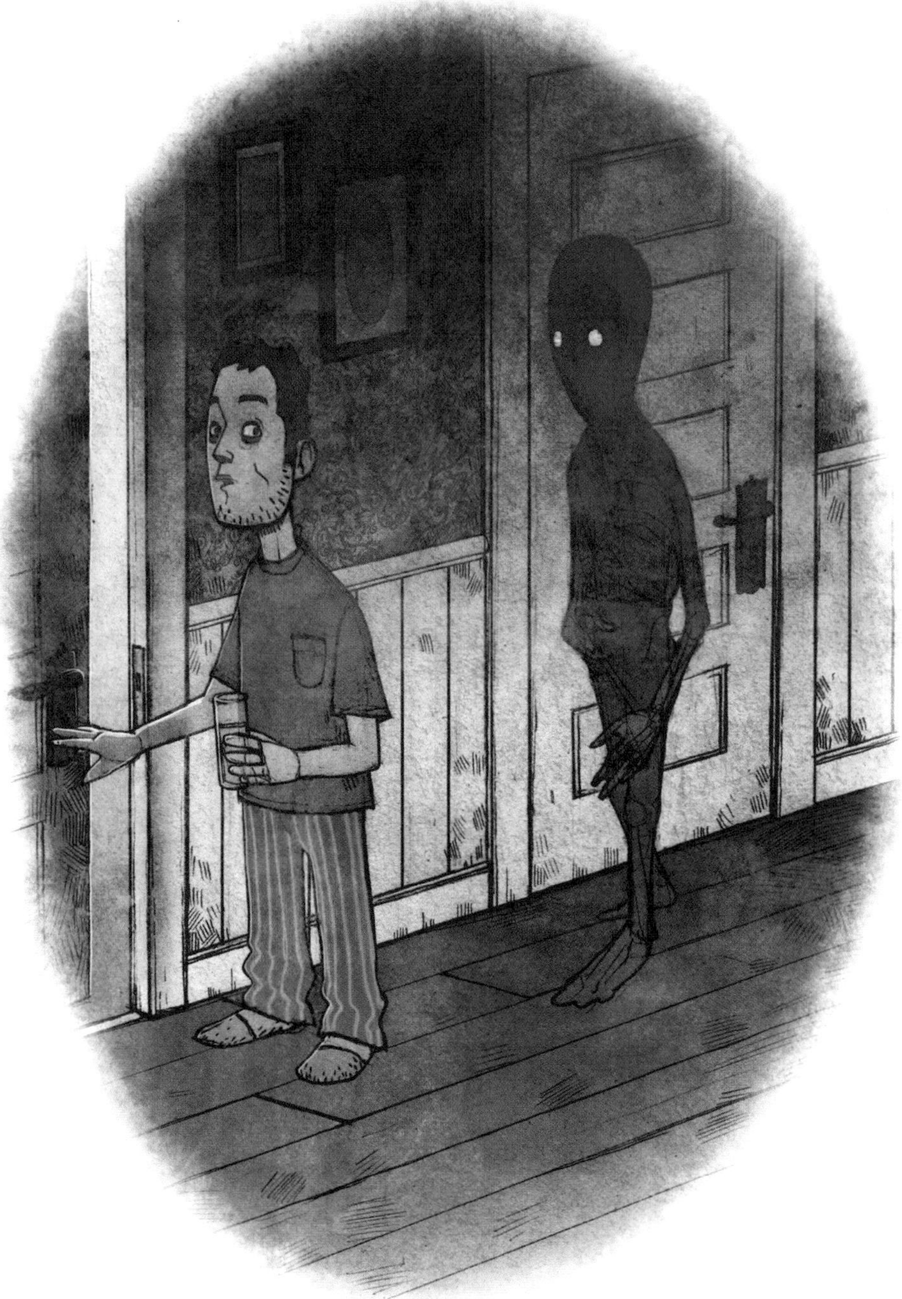

the mirror was already here when we moved in

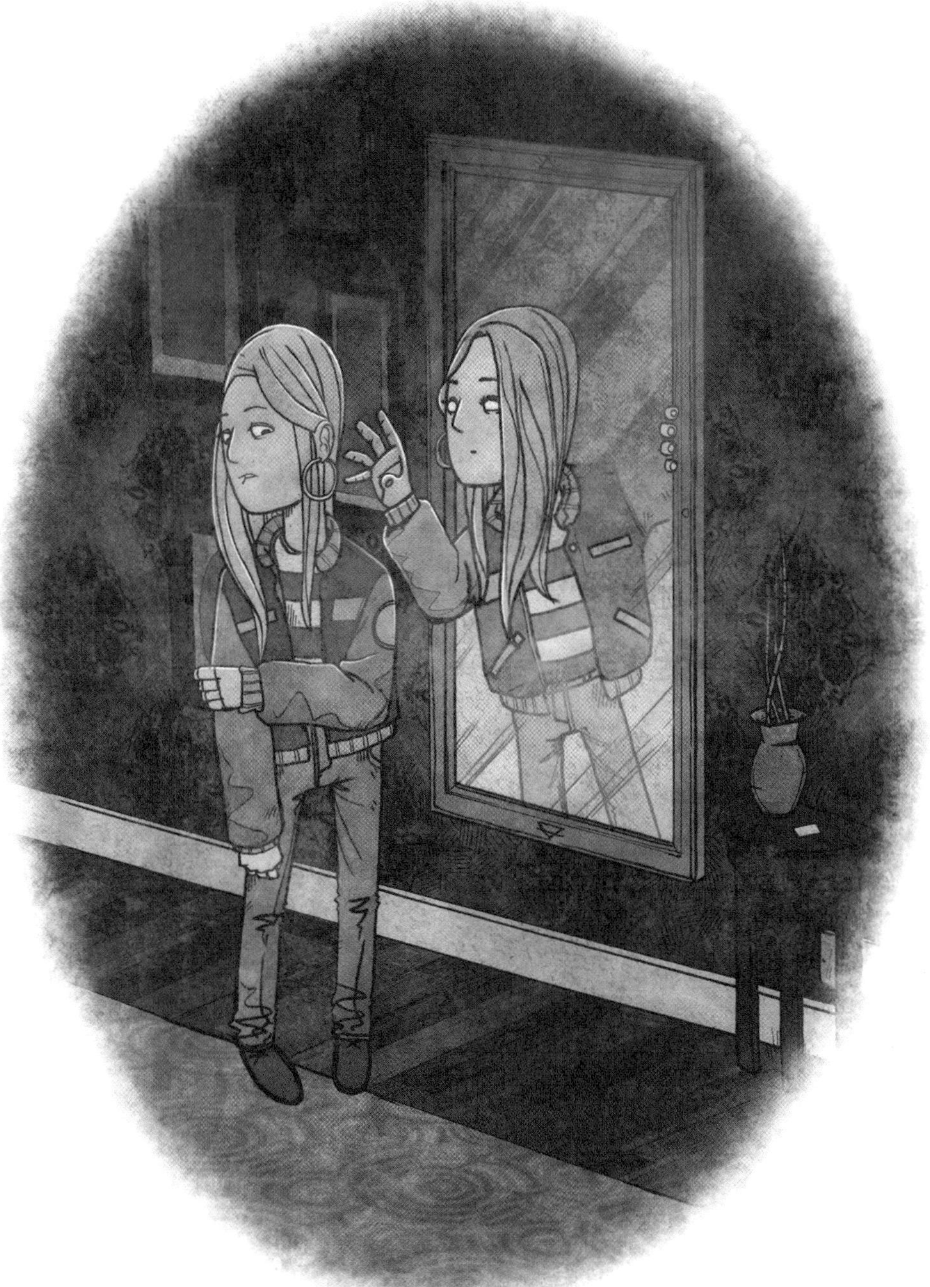

the more i read of this town's past, the worse it gets

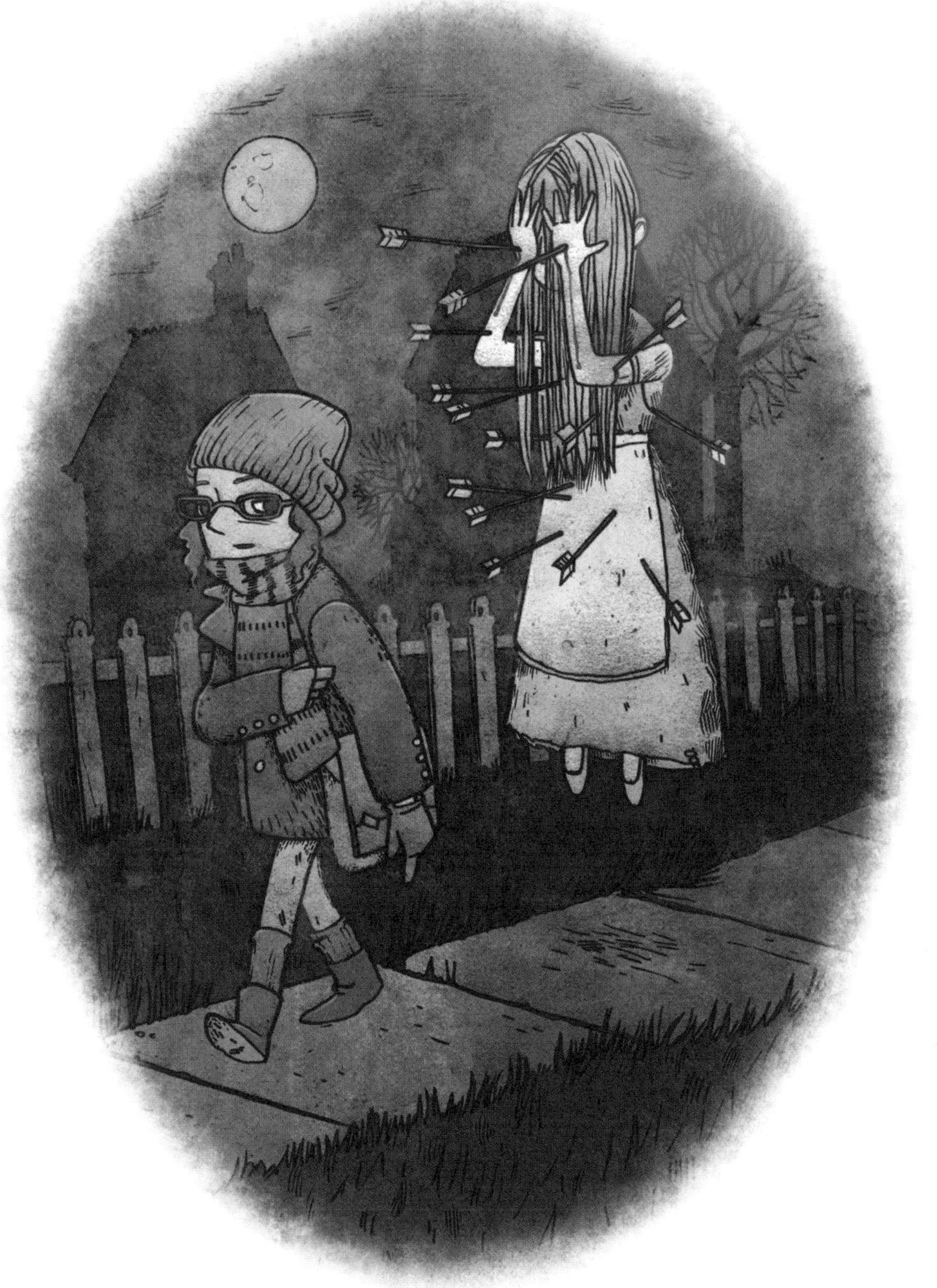

he got the job after the previous guard disappeared

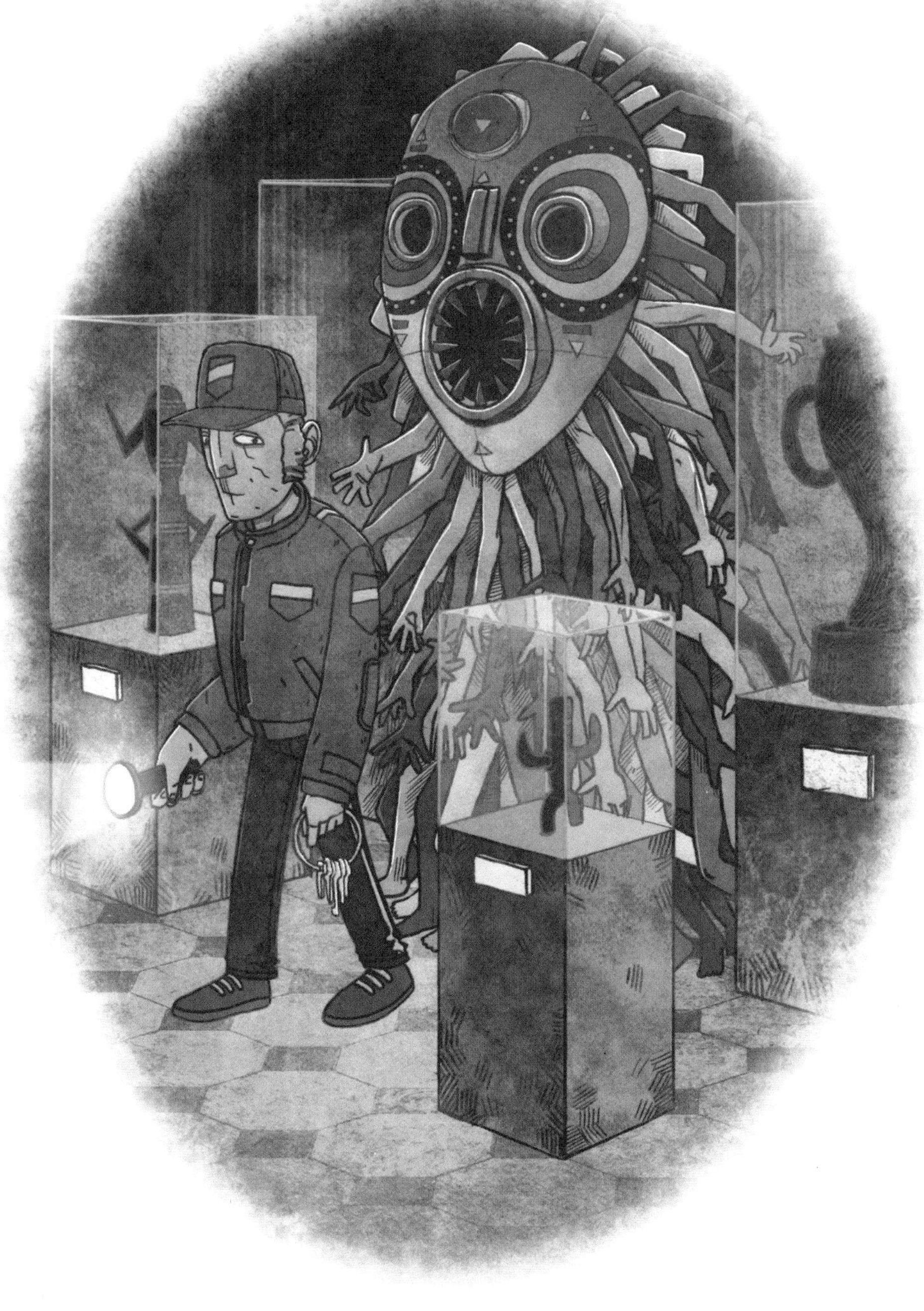

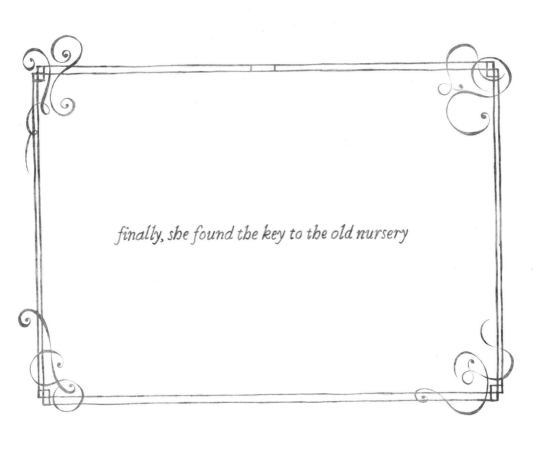

finally, she found the key to the old nursery

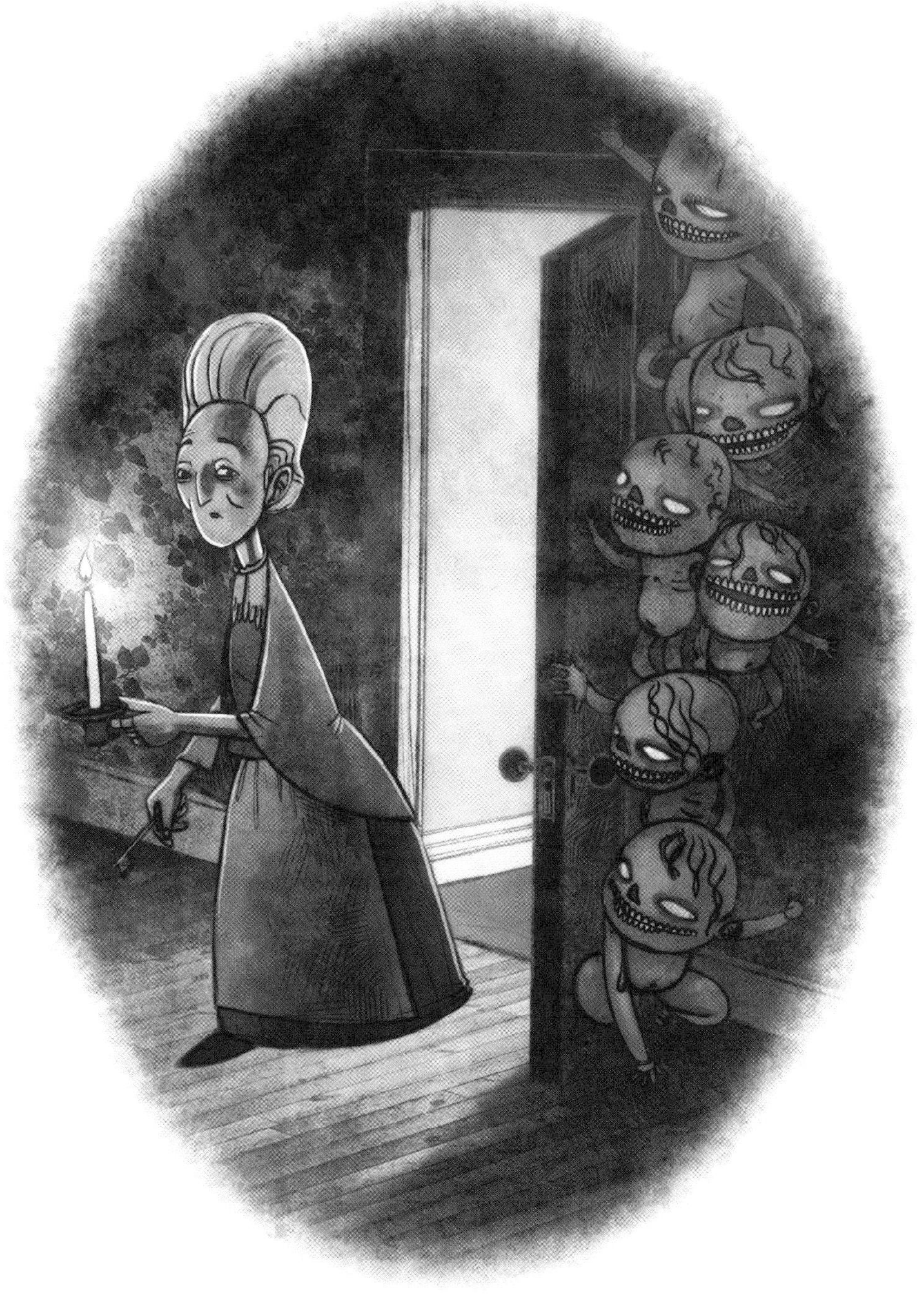

i should have visited more often

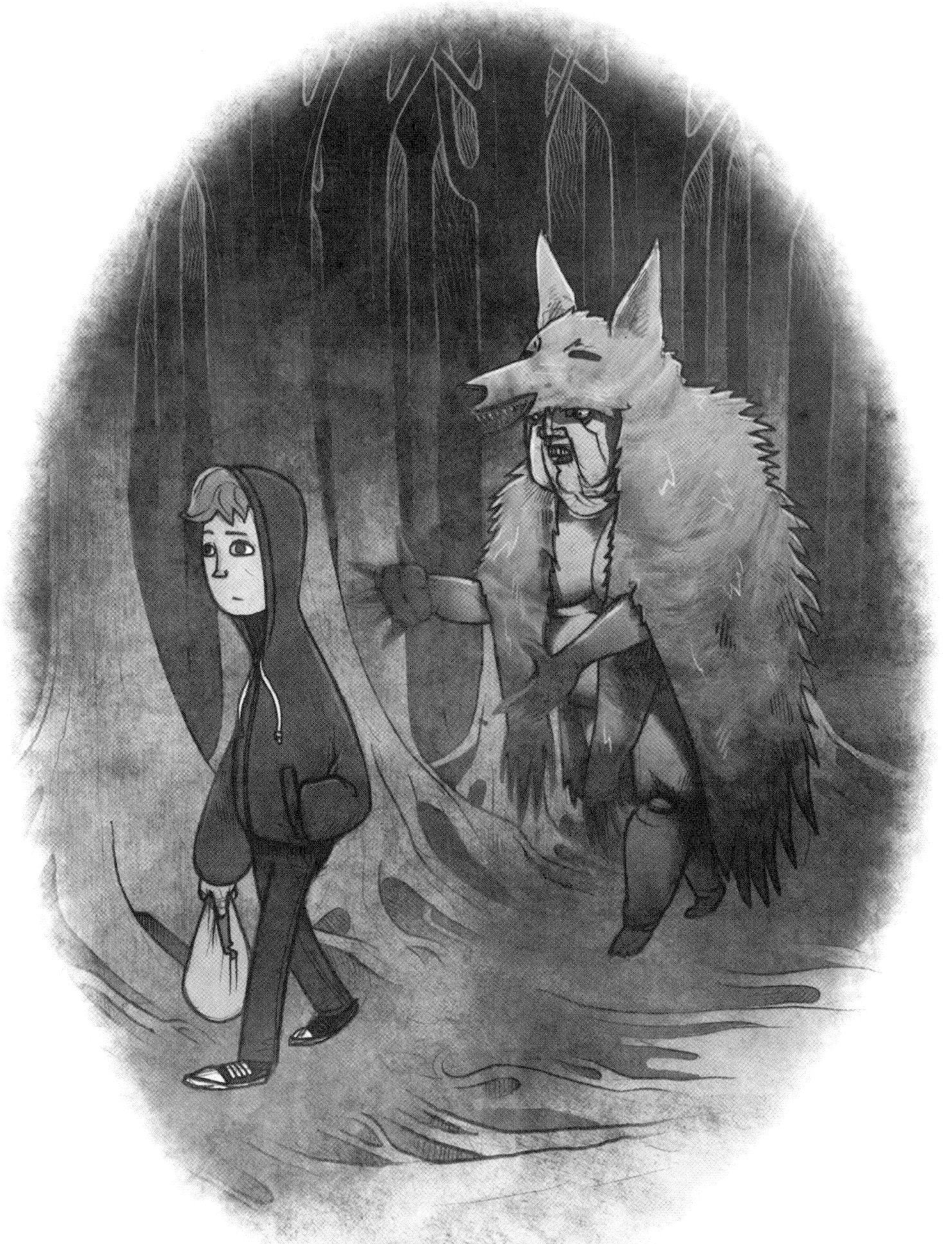

the statue was where the old man had said it would be

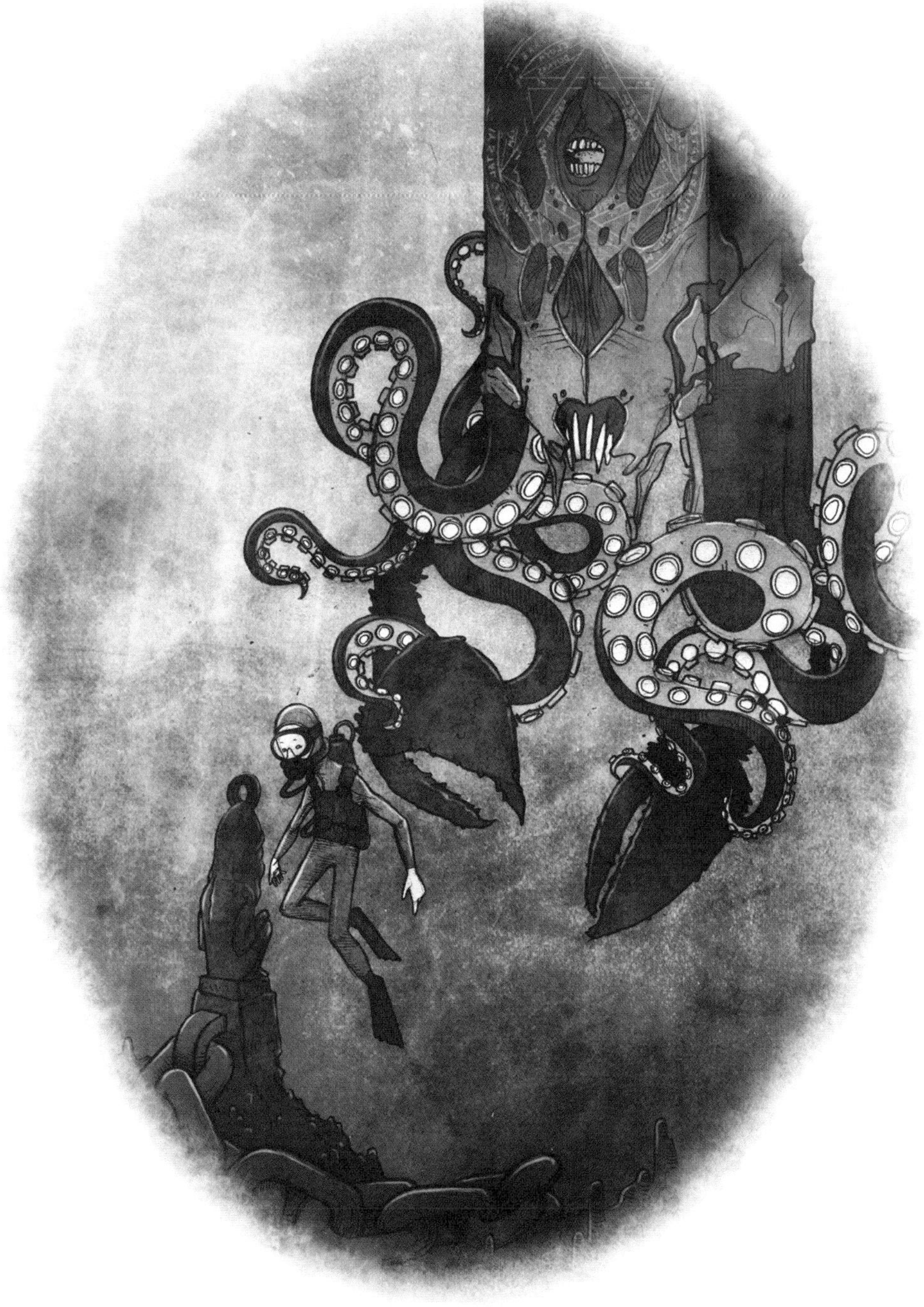

the book had described himself, his room,
his chair and it

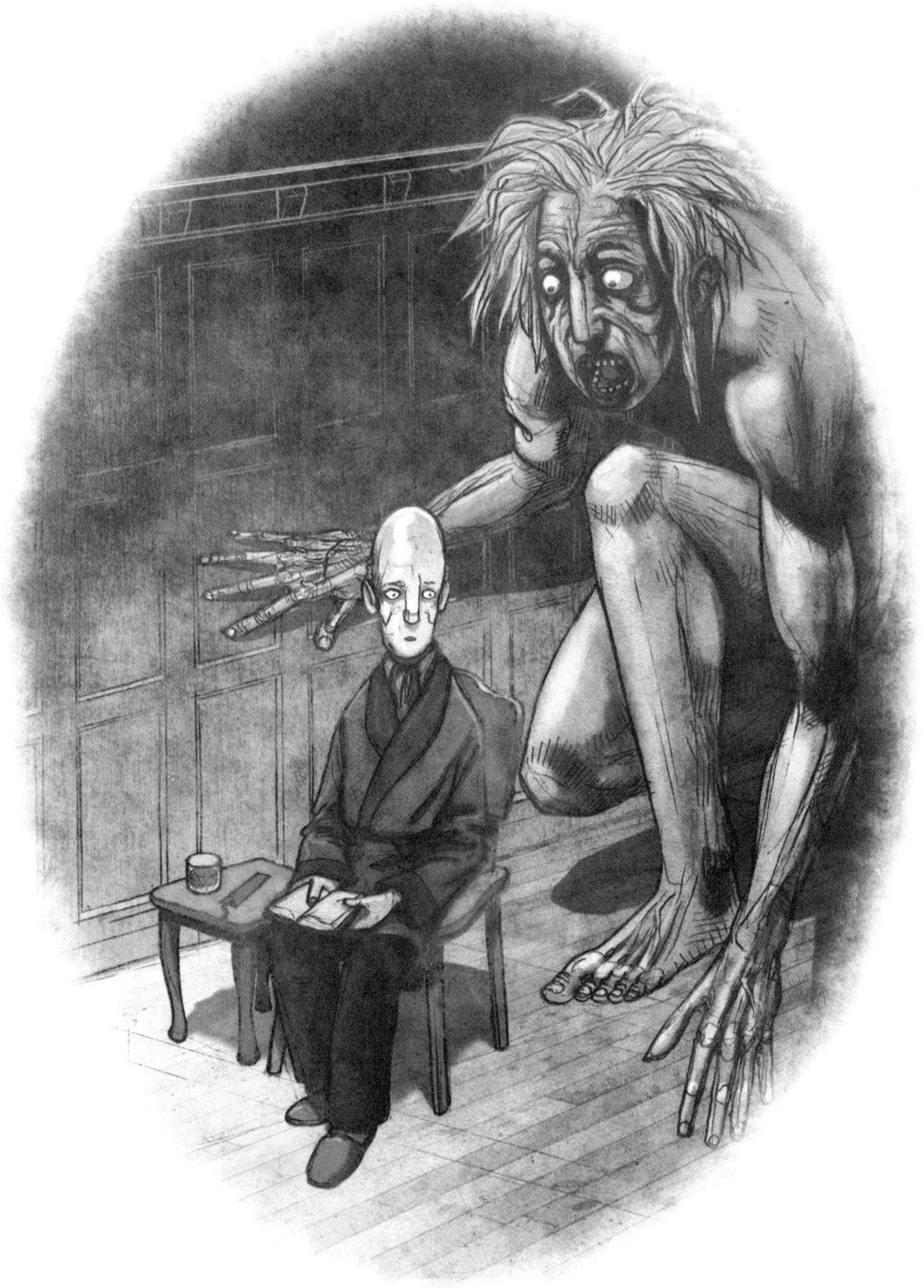

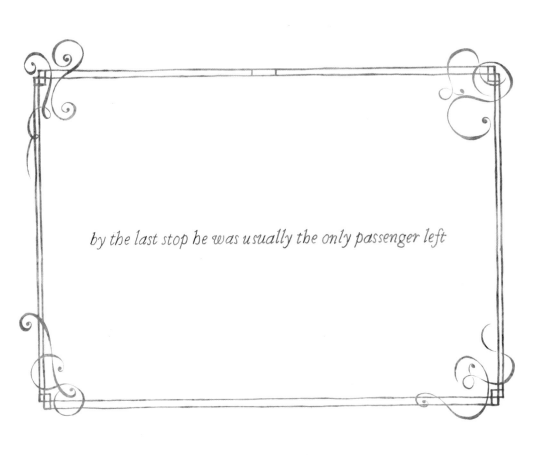

by the last stop he was usually the only passenger left

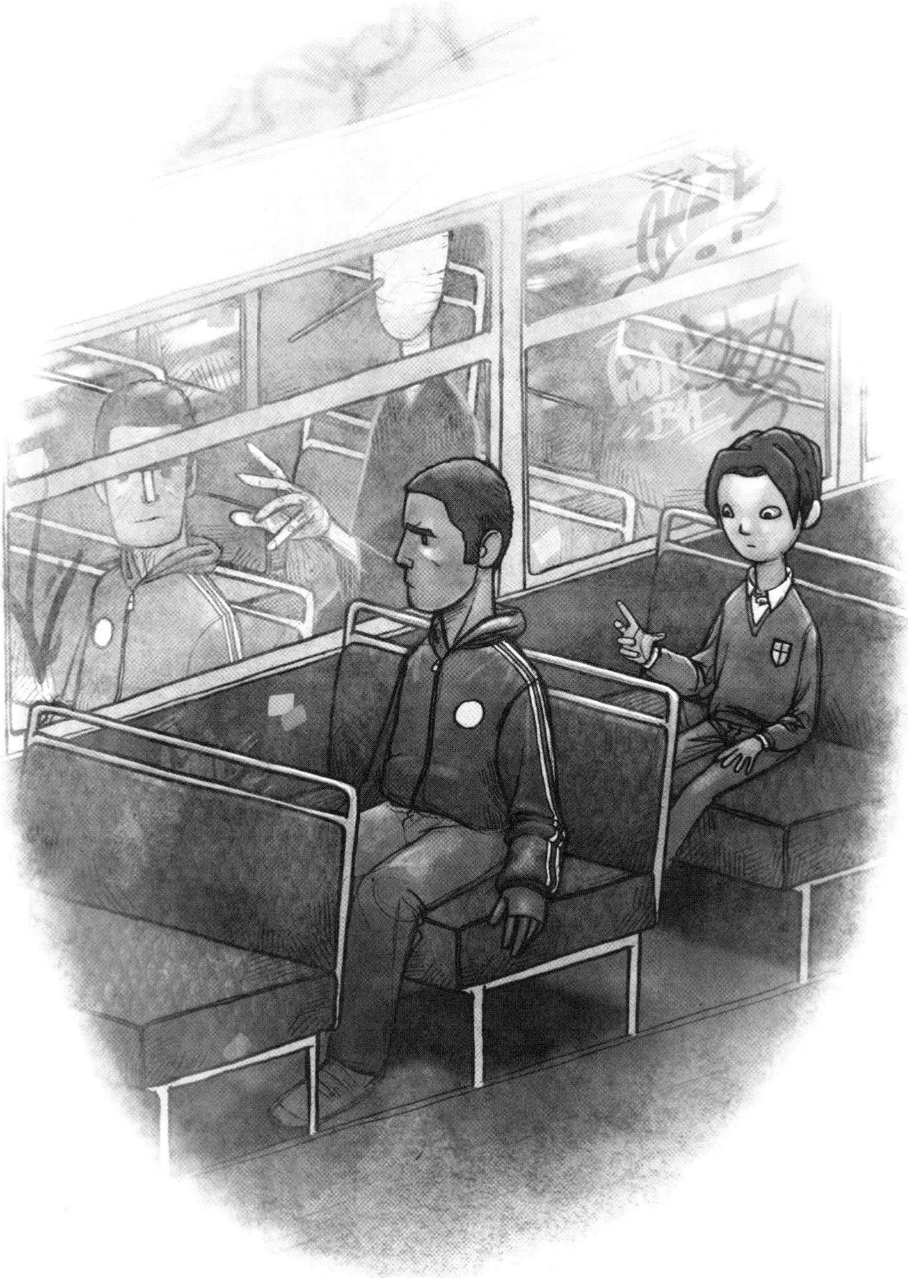

how long had it been since anyone was down here?

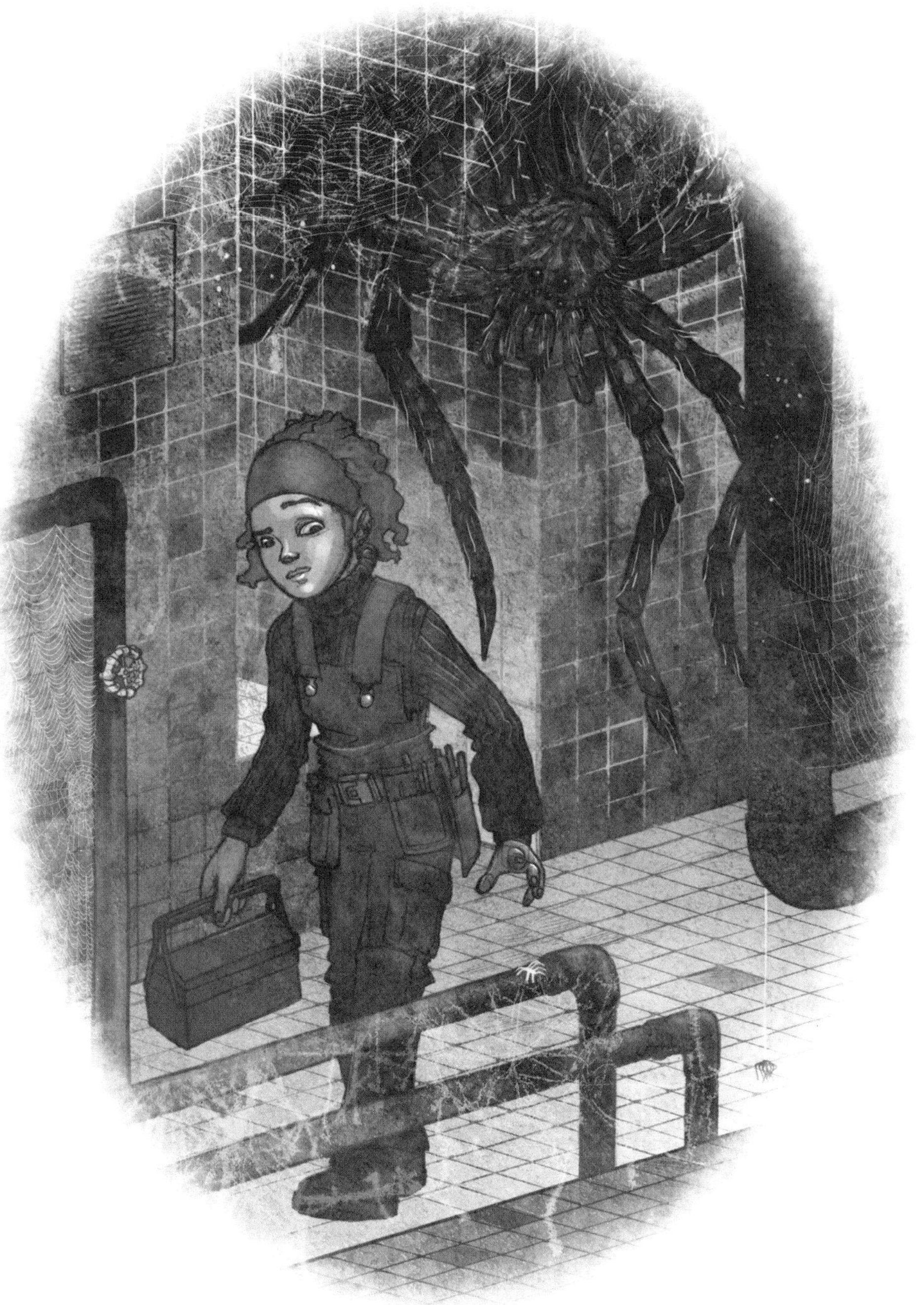

he had only wanted to look inside...
it was just full of dust

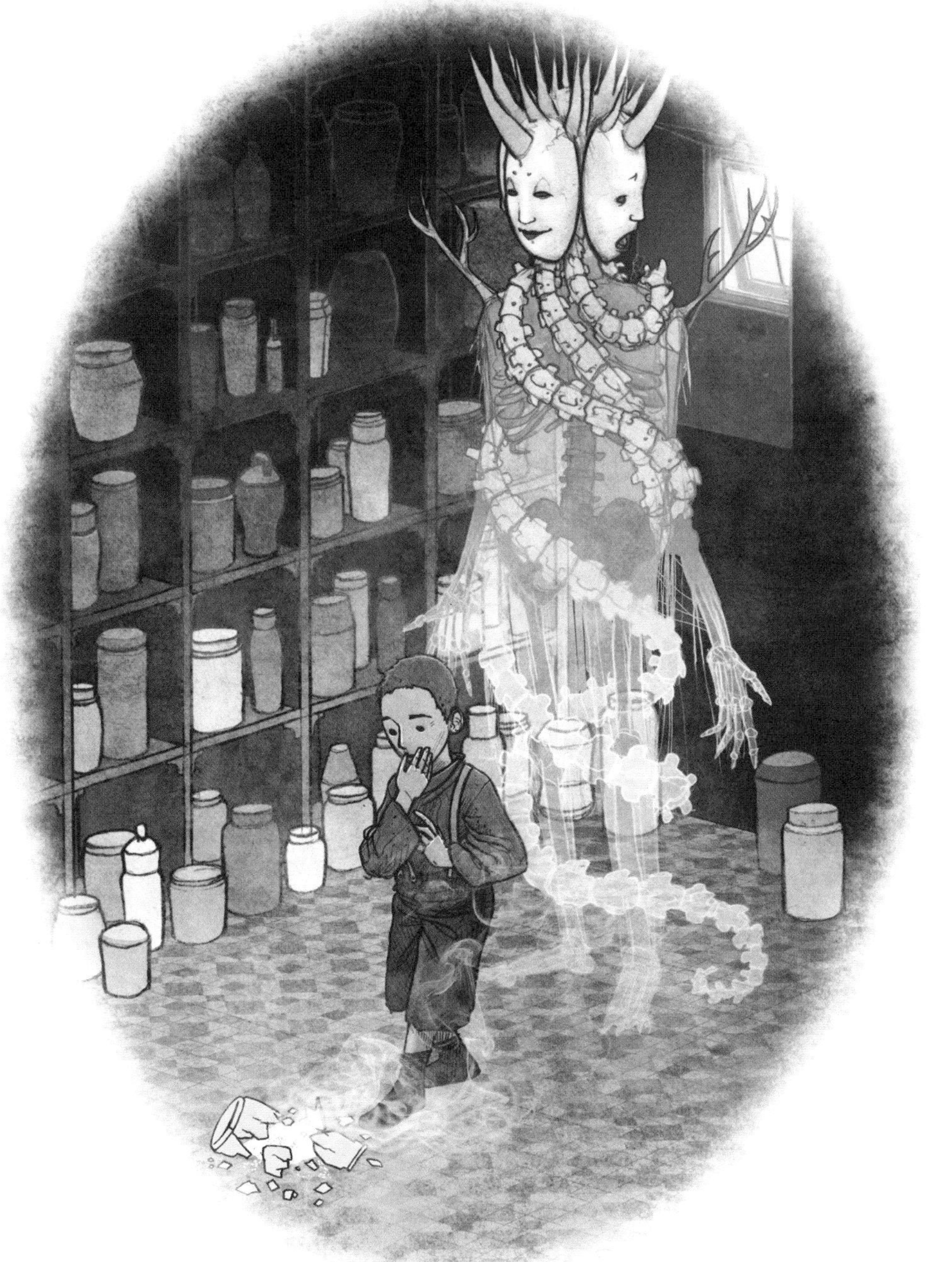

five for silver,
six for gold

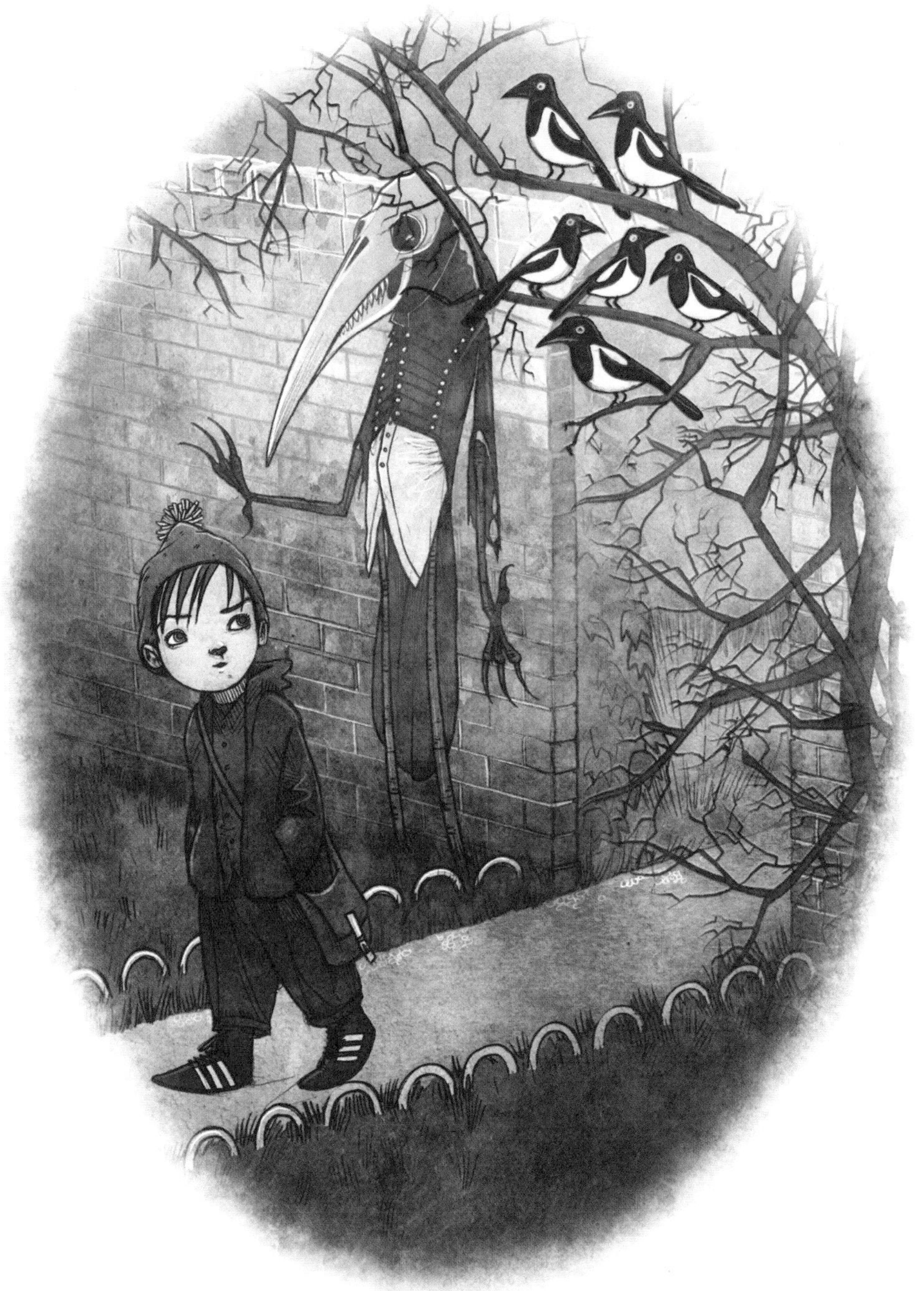

this had been her room

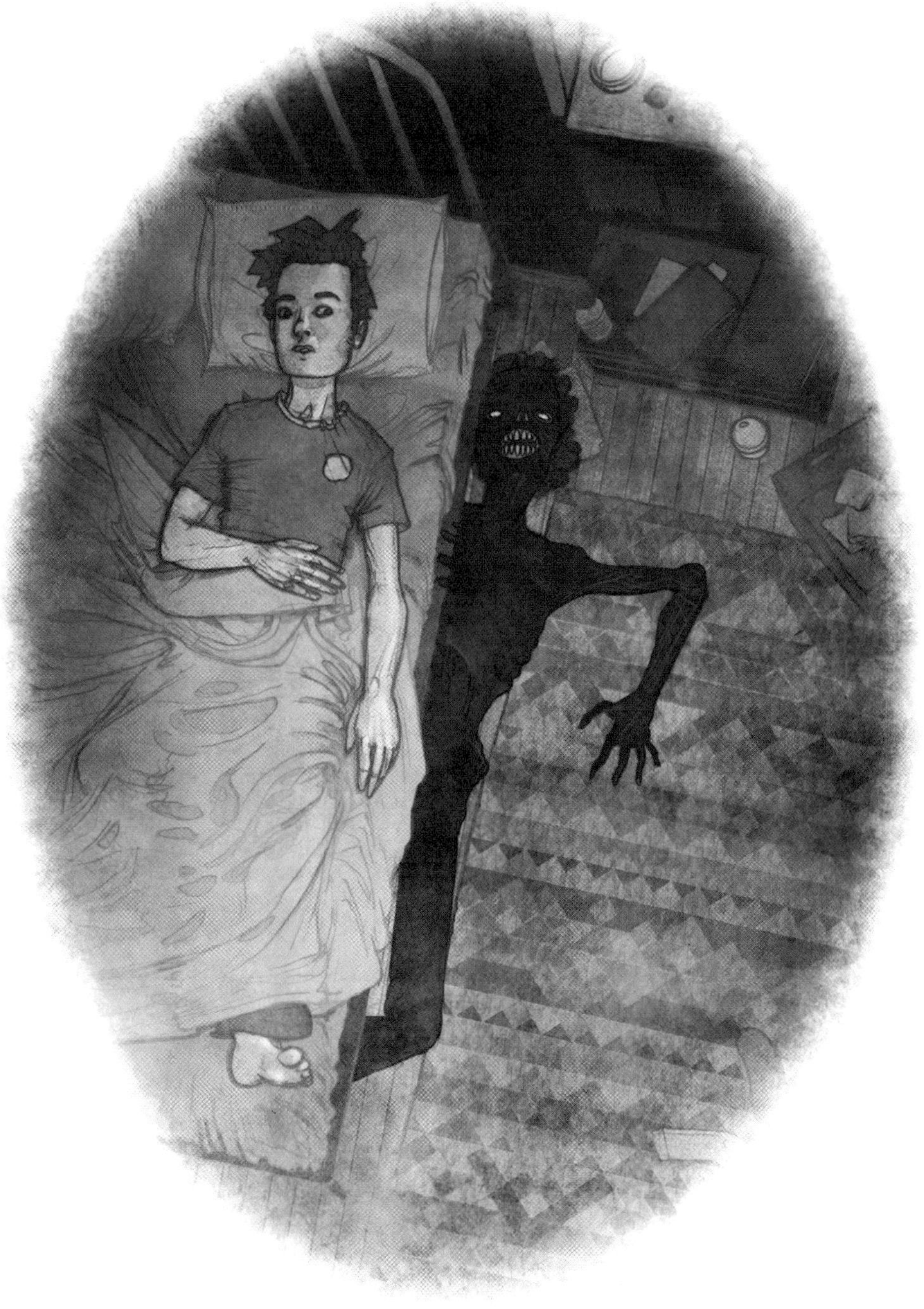

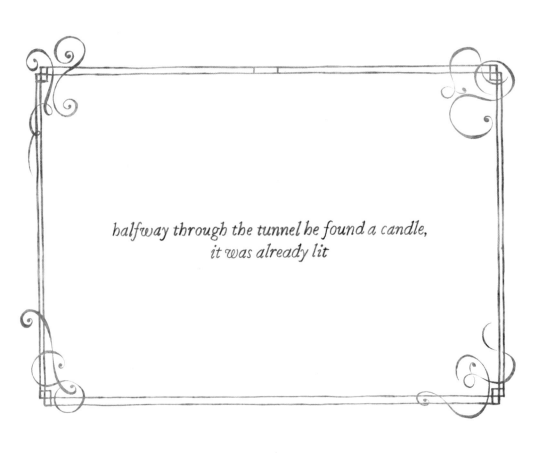

halfway through the tunnel he found a candle,
it was already lit

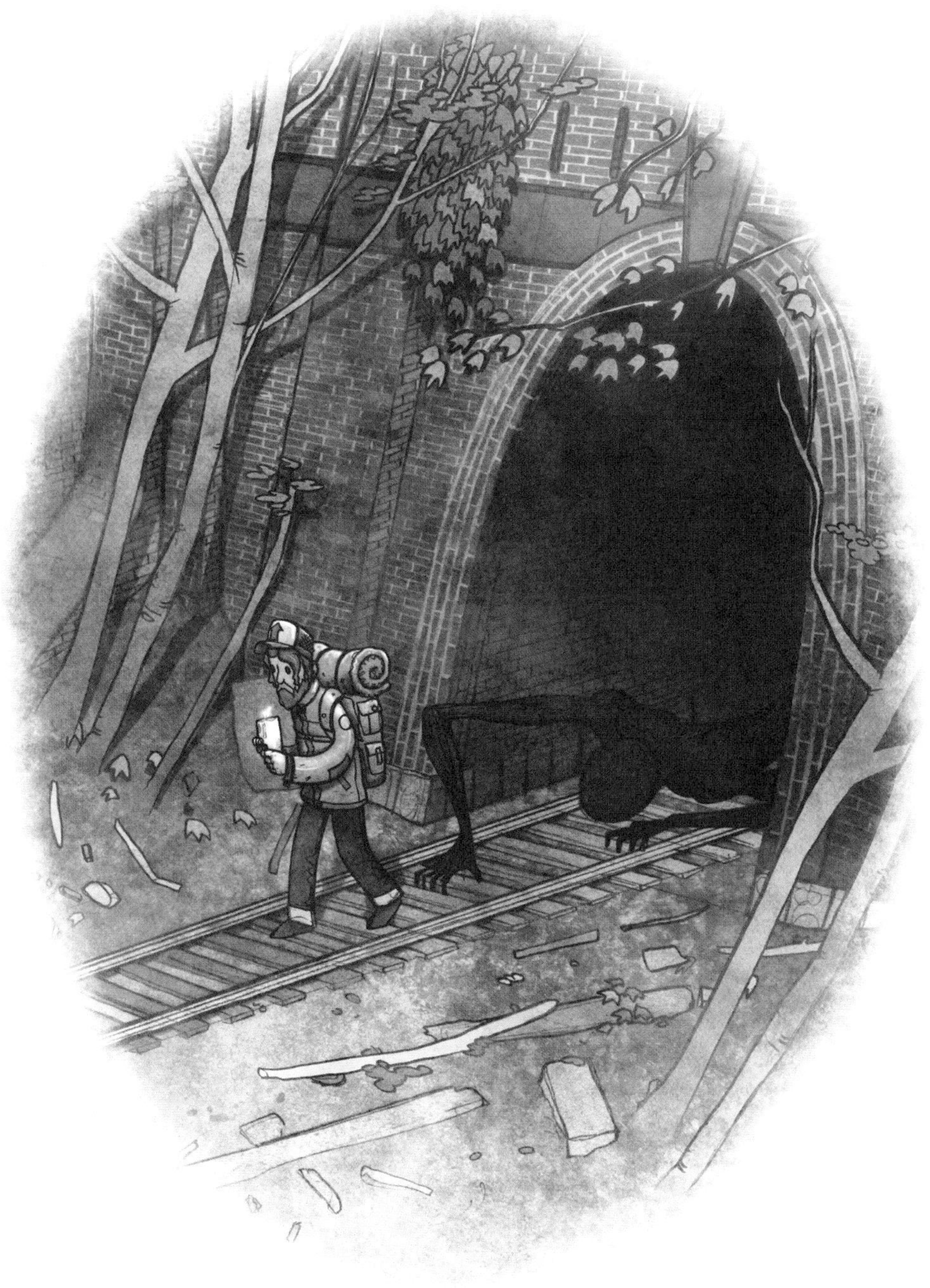

she knew it would work.
she did not know what it would make visible

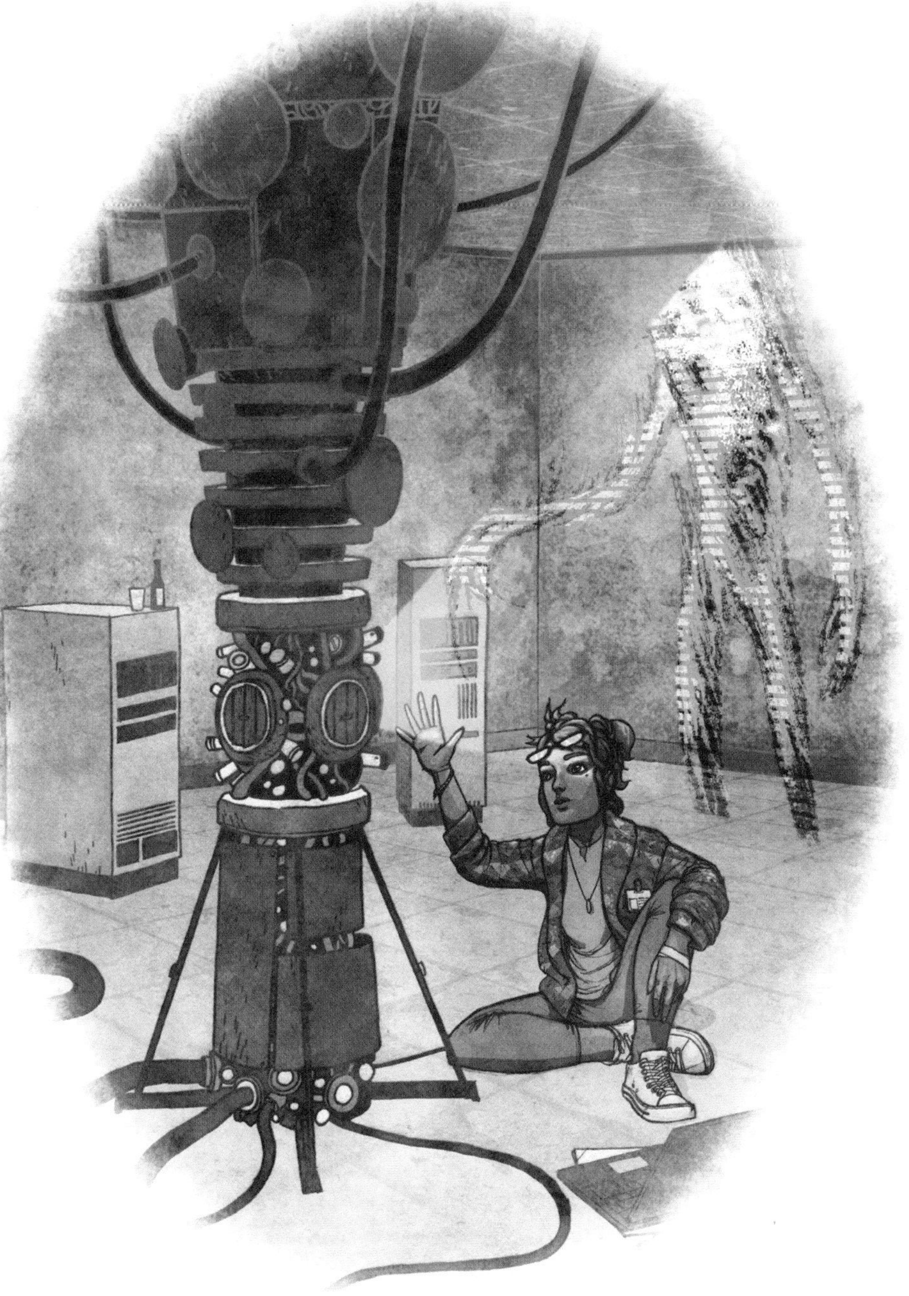

i decided to stay up all night.
i would just avoid those dreams altogether

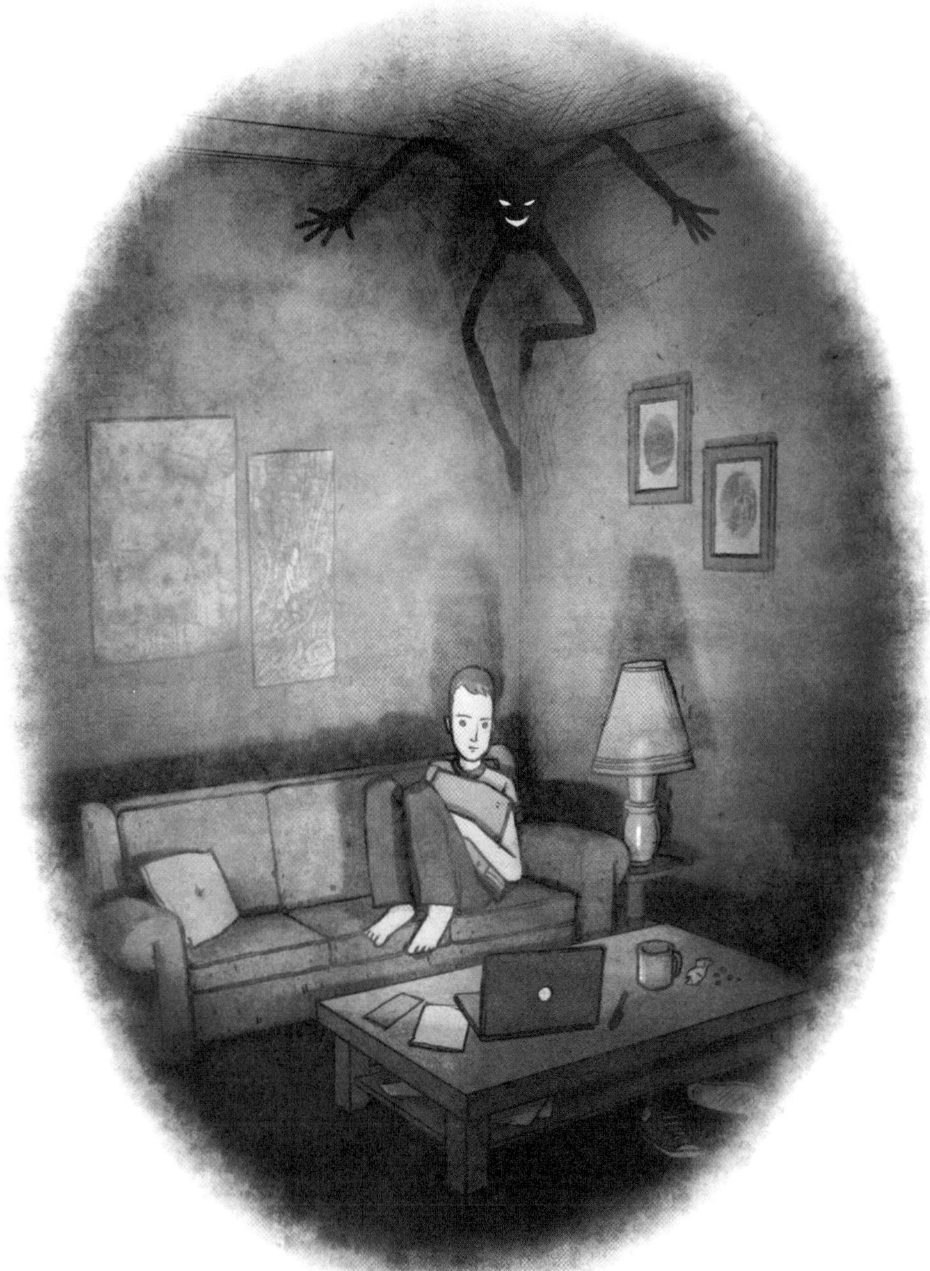

stupid hospital thought it was so scary.
tonight she would show it who's boss and walk it alone

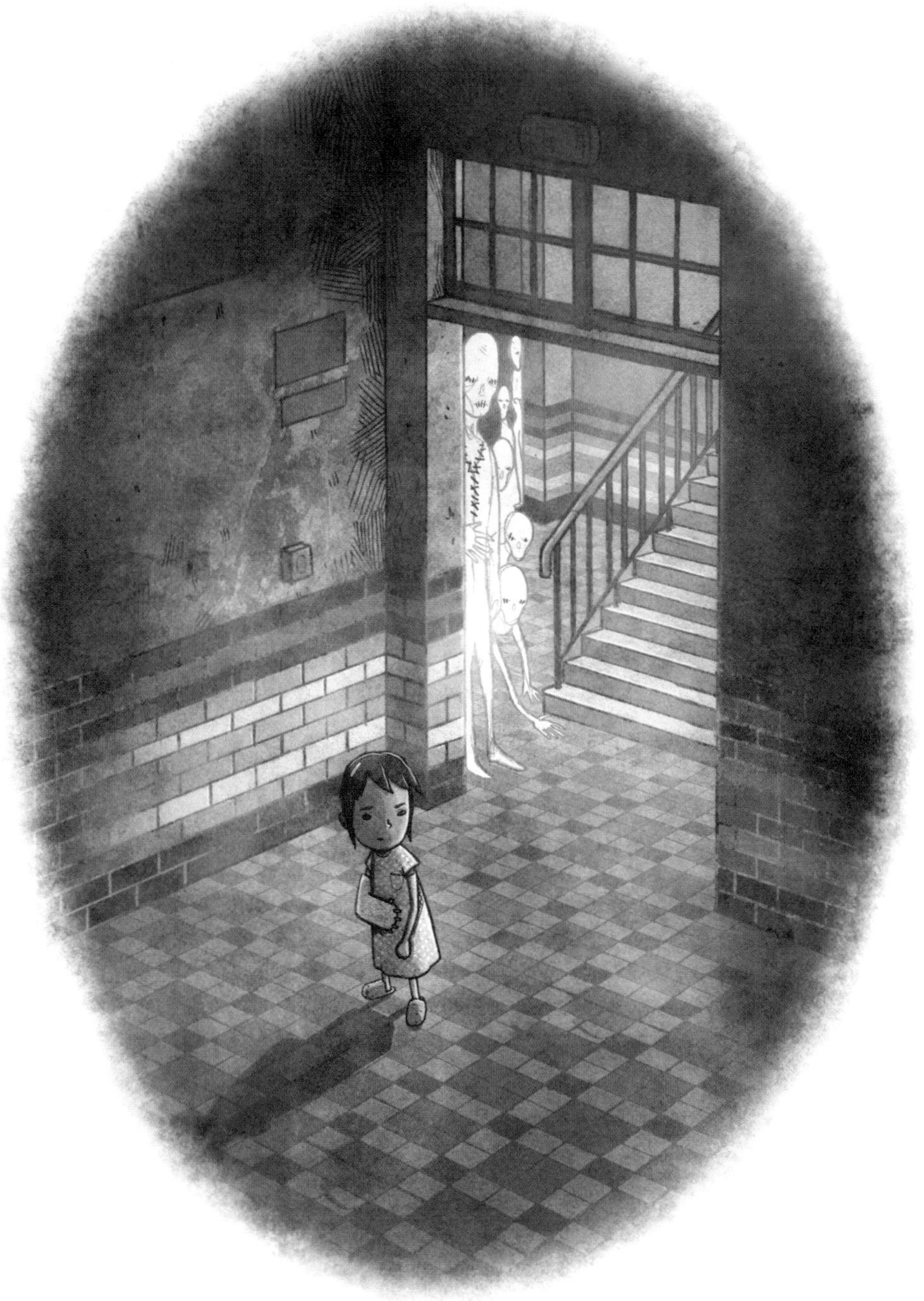

no one else even lived in the building anymore
yet other steps always echoed up the stairwell
beside her own

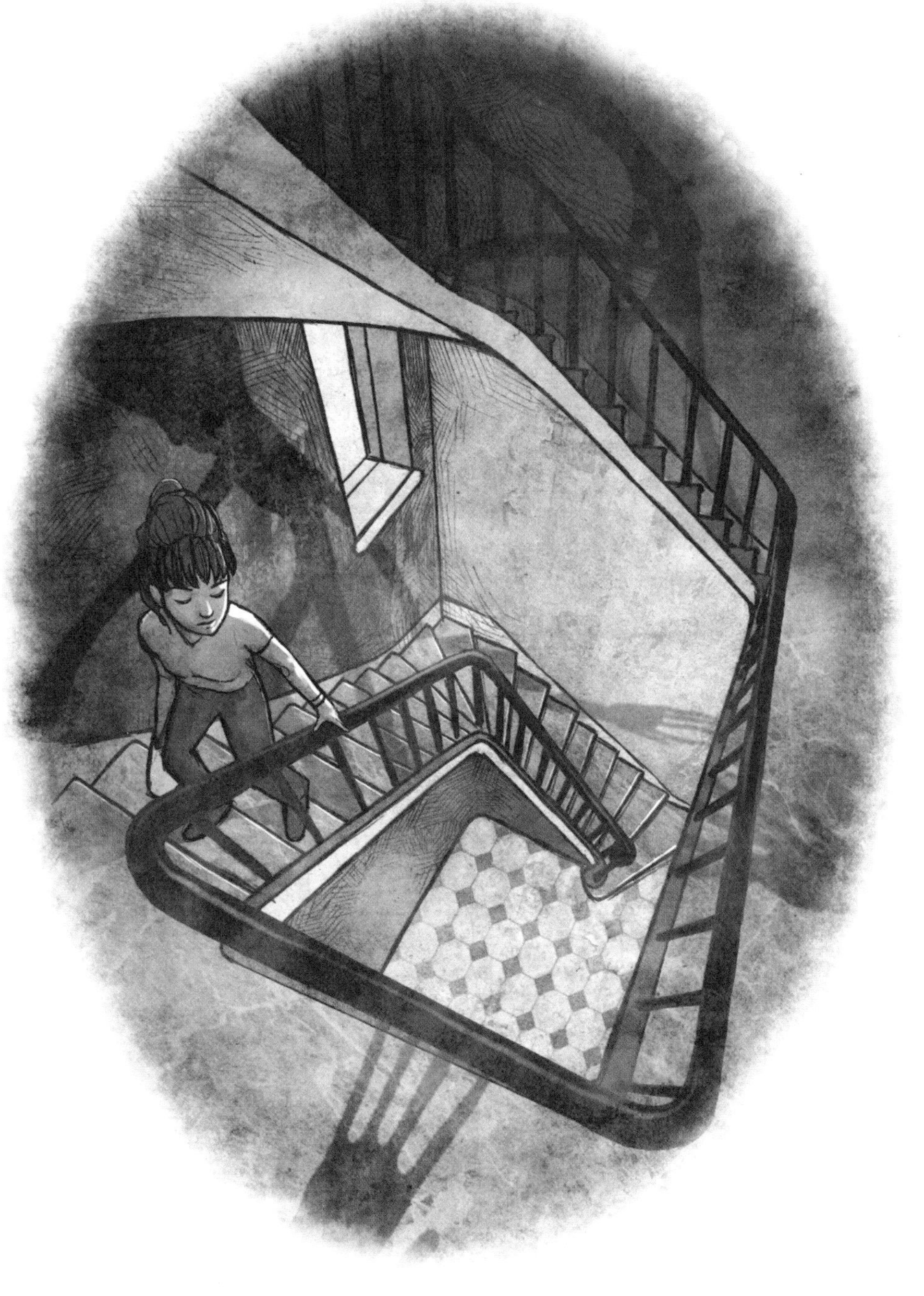

first she will find somewhere secluded
and split herself in two,
then she will come

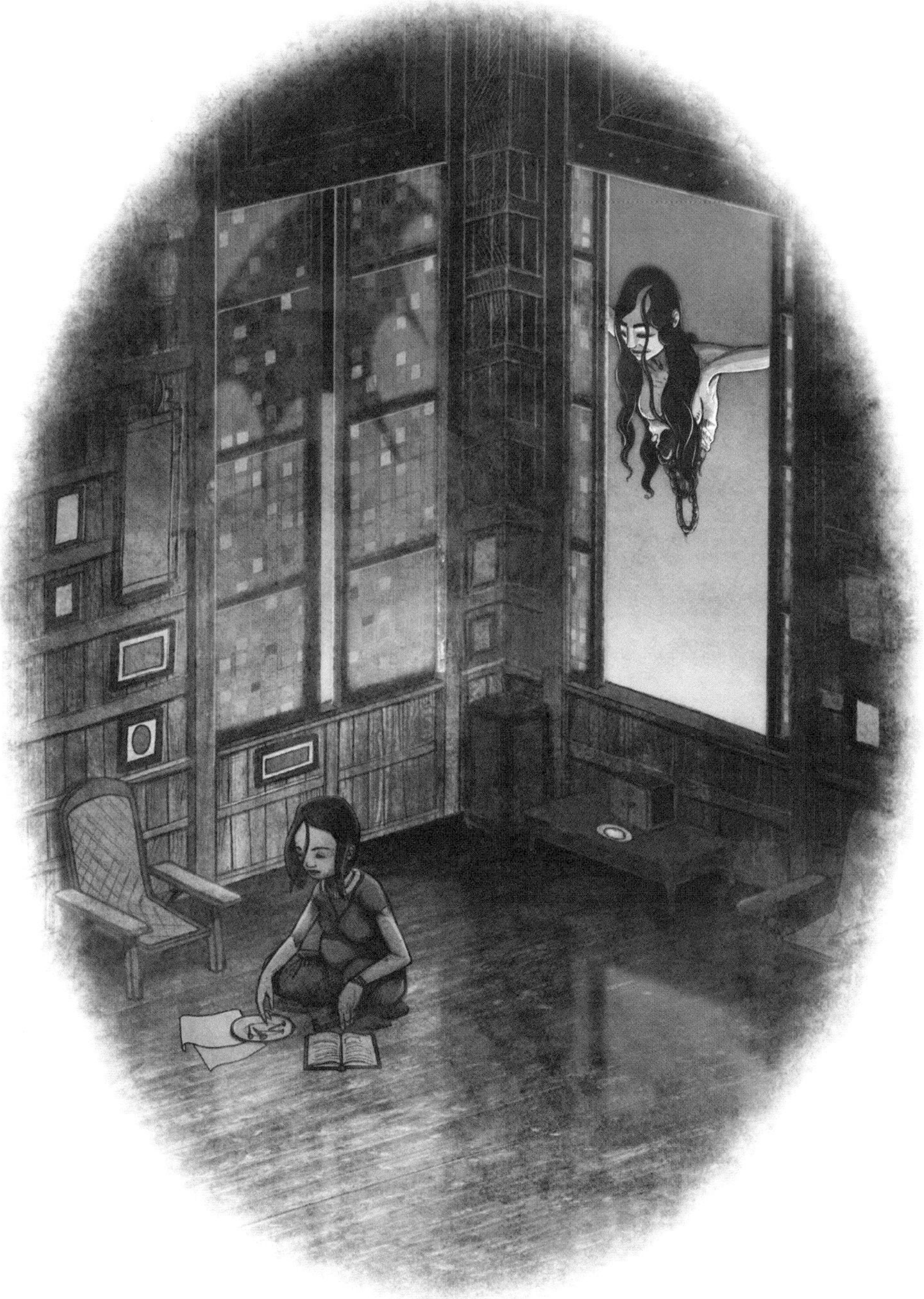

*she noticed the streetlights popping off one by one
as she walked under them, as if they were waiting for her*

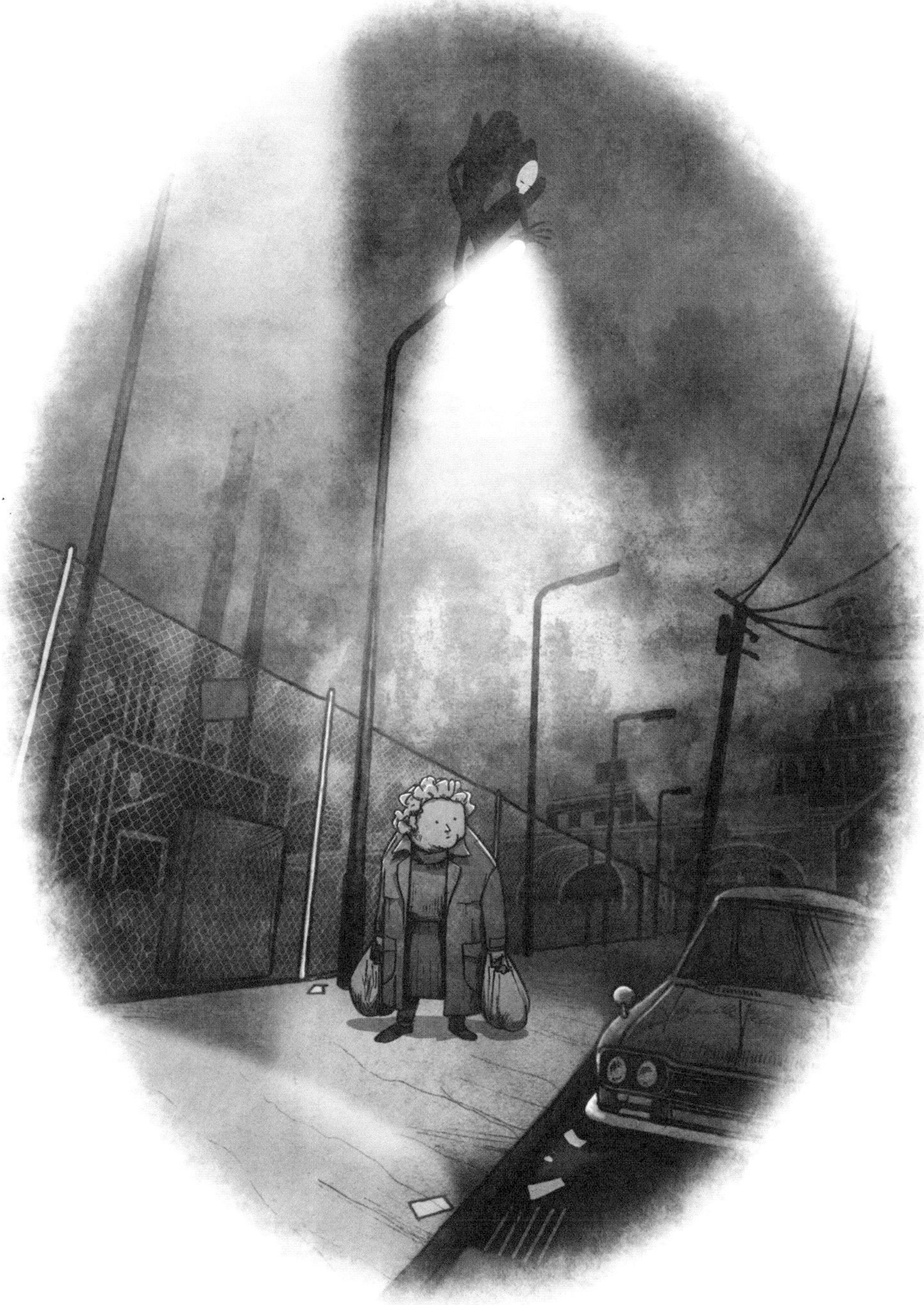

the wind screamed.
that night the empty house would be full of sound
as it strained to keep out the storm

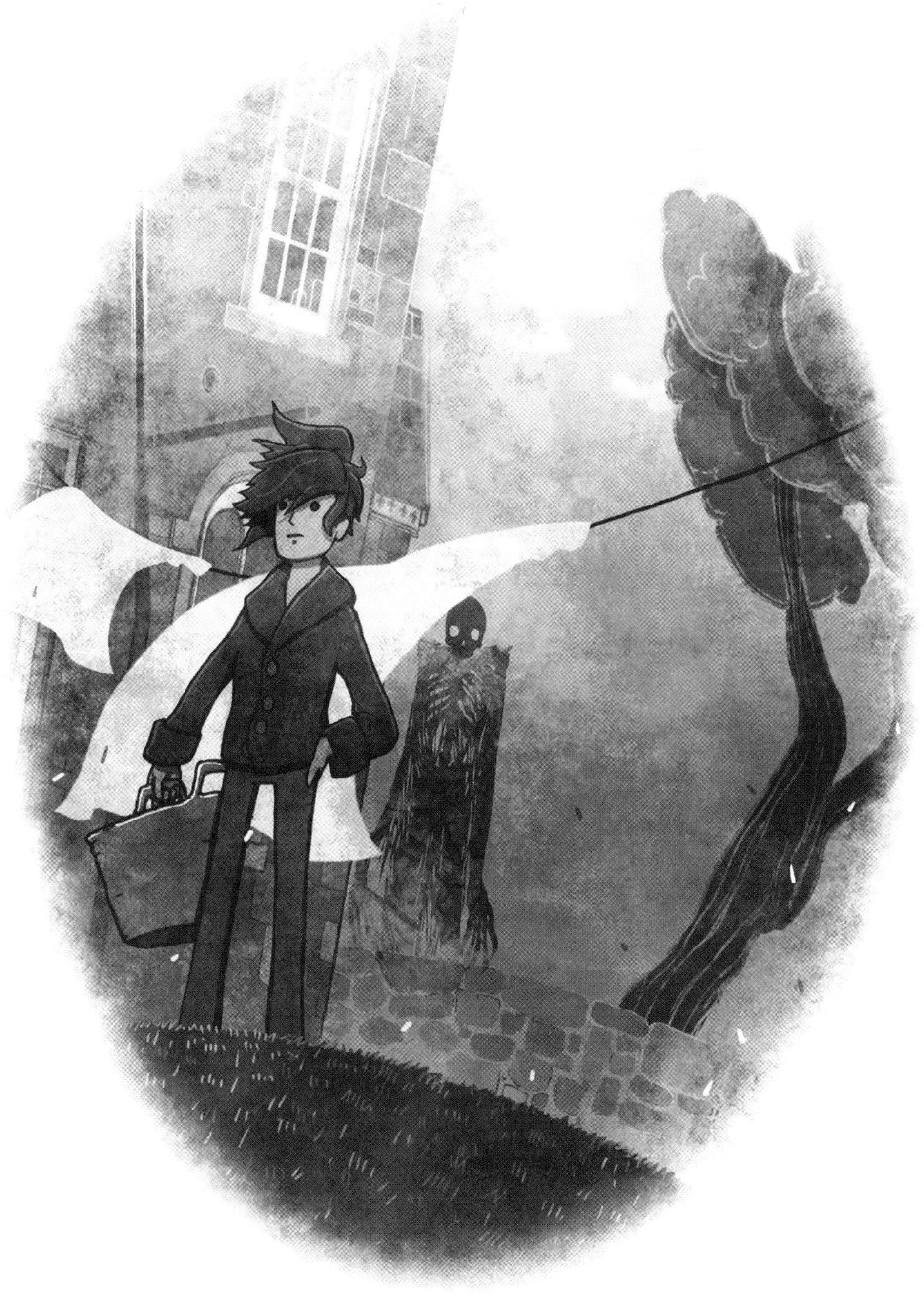

it was a day to spend indoors

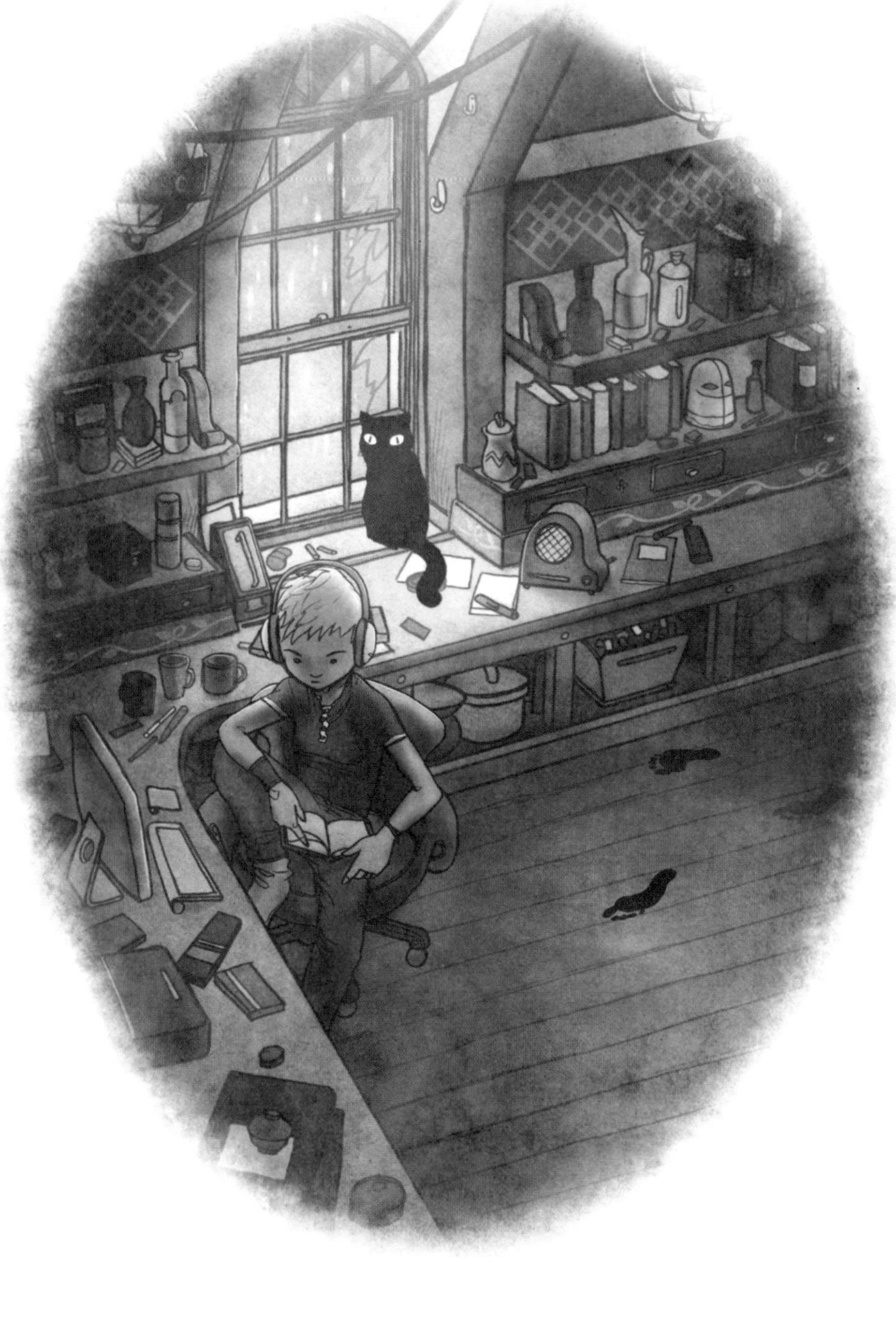

i swear, one day these stairs will be the death of me

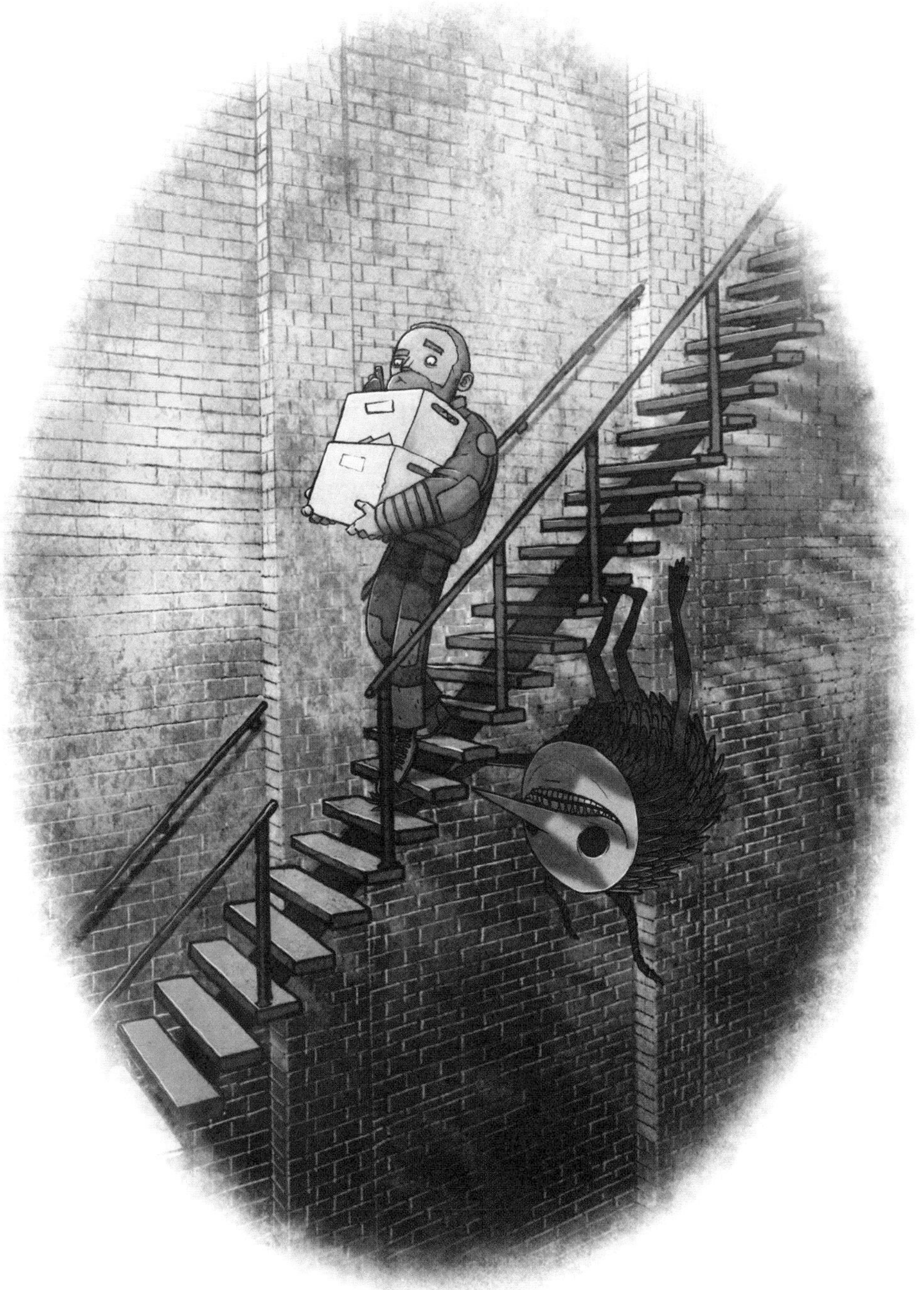

his rickety digs
looked like they hadn't seen an owner in years,
never mind a paying guest

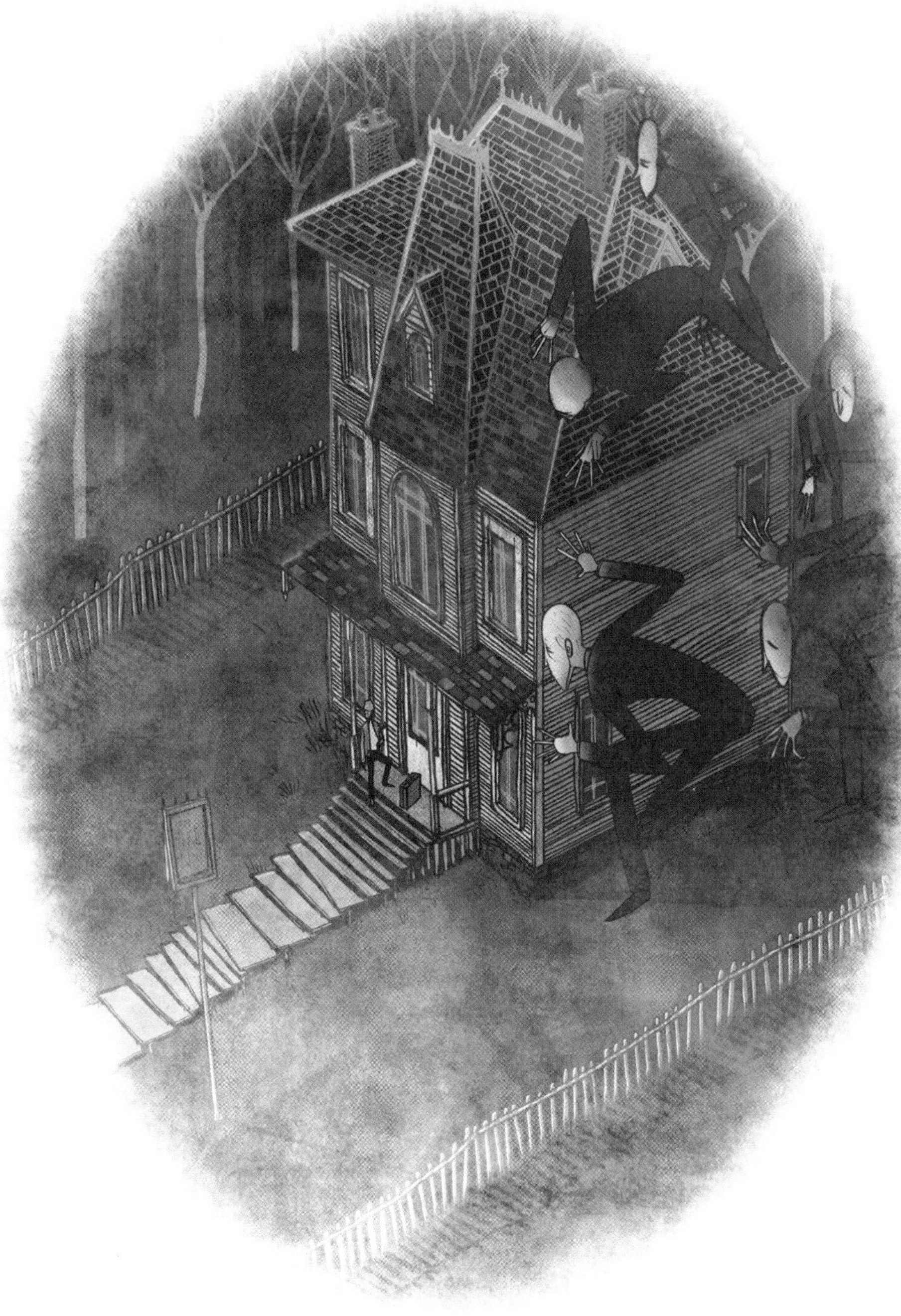

would he ever get used to the place,
ever call it home?
countless others had over the years

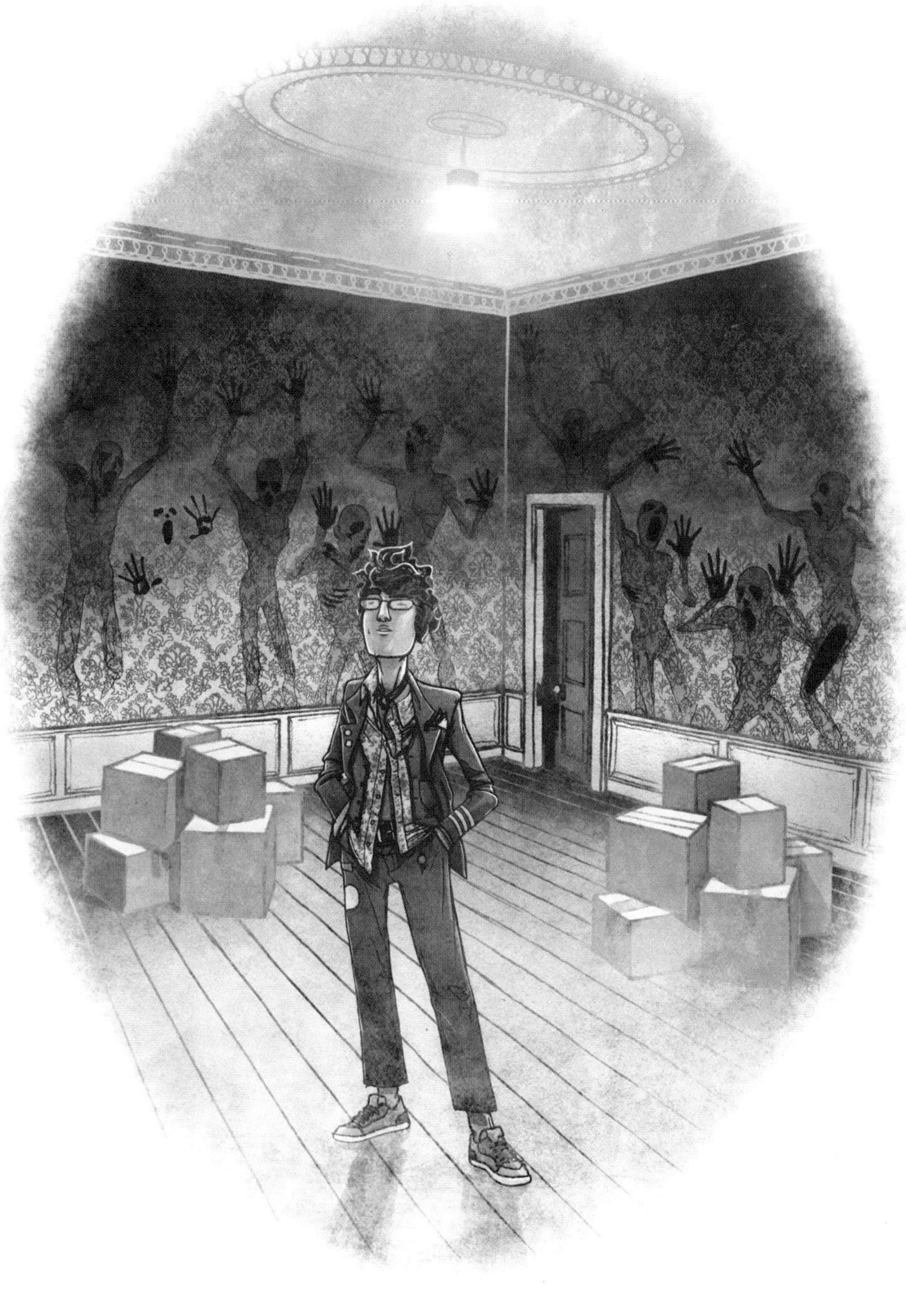

the new school was cold and vast. and it was empty.
where were the other pupils?
and where were the teachers?

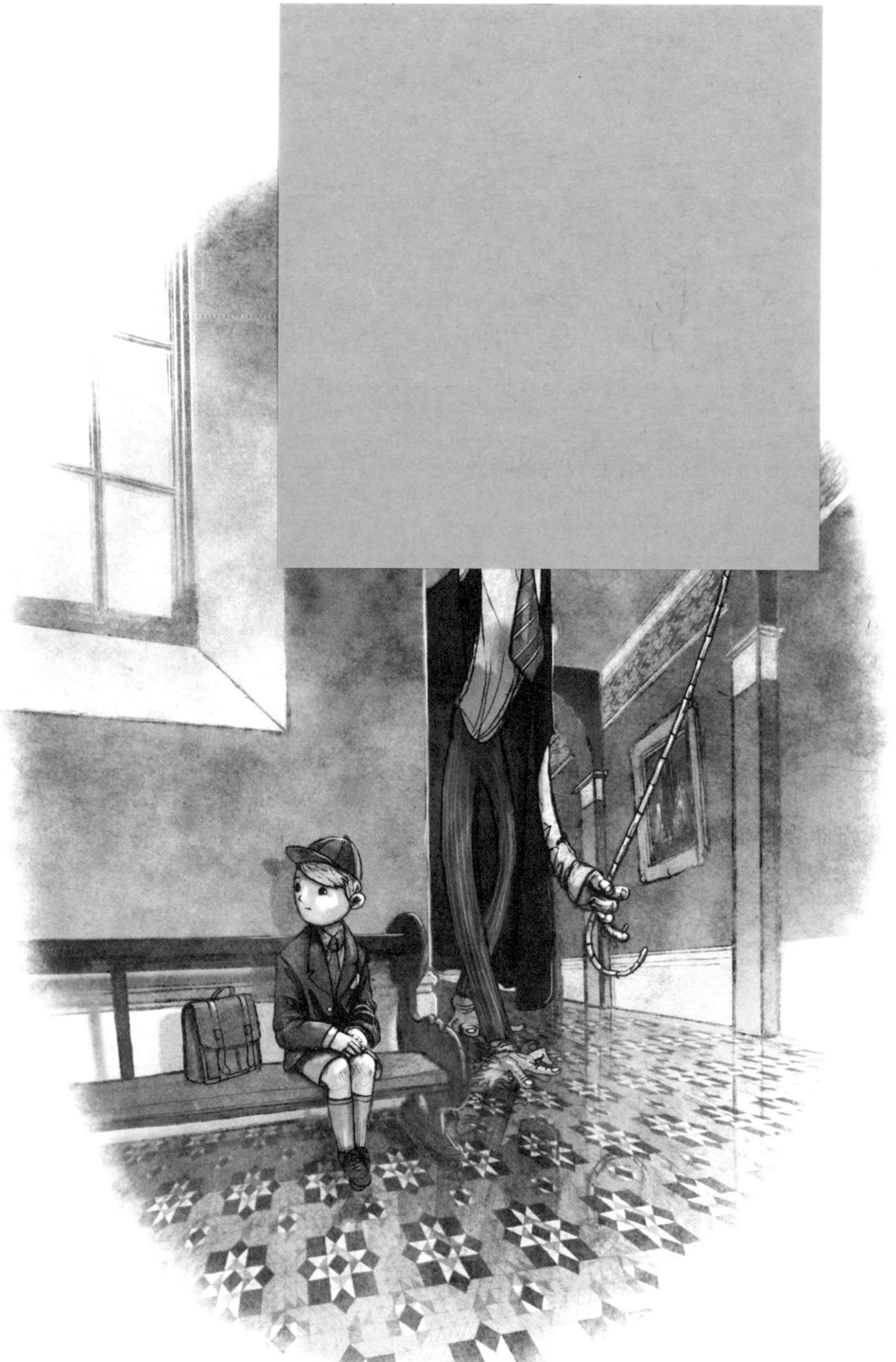

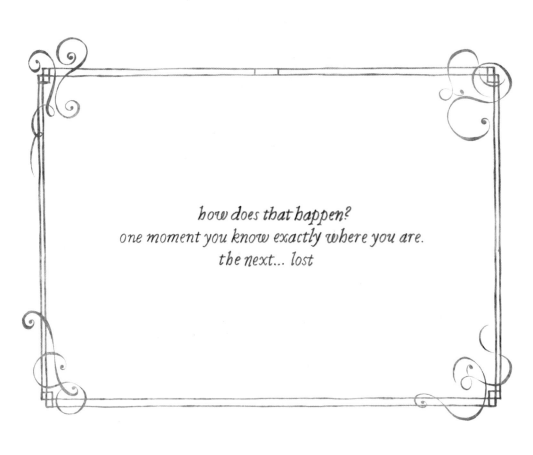

how does that happen?
one moment you know exactly where you are.
the next... lost

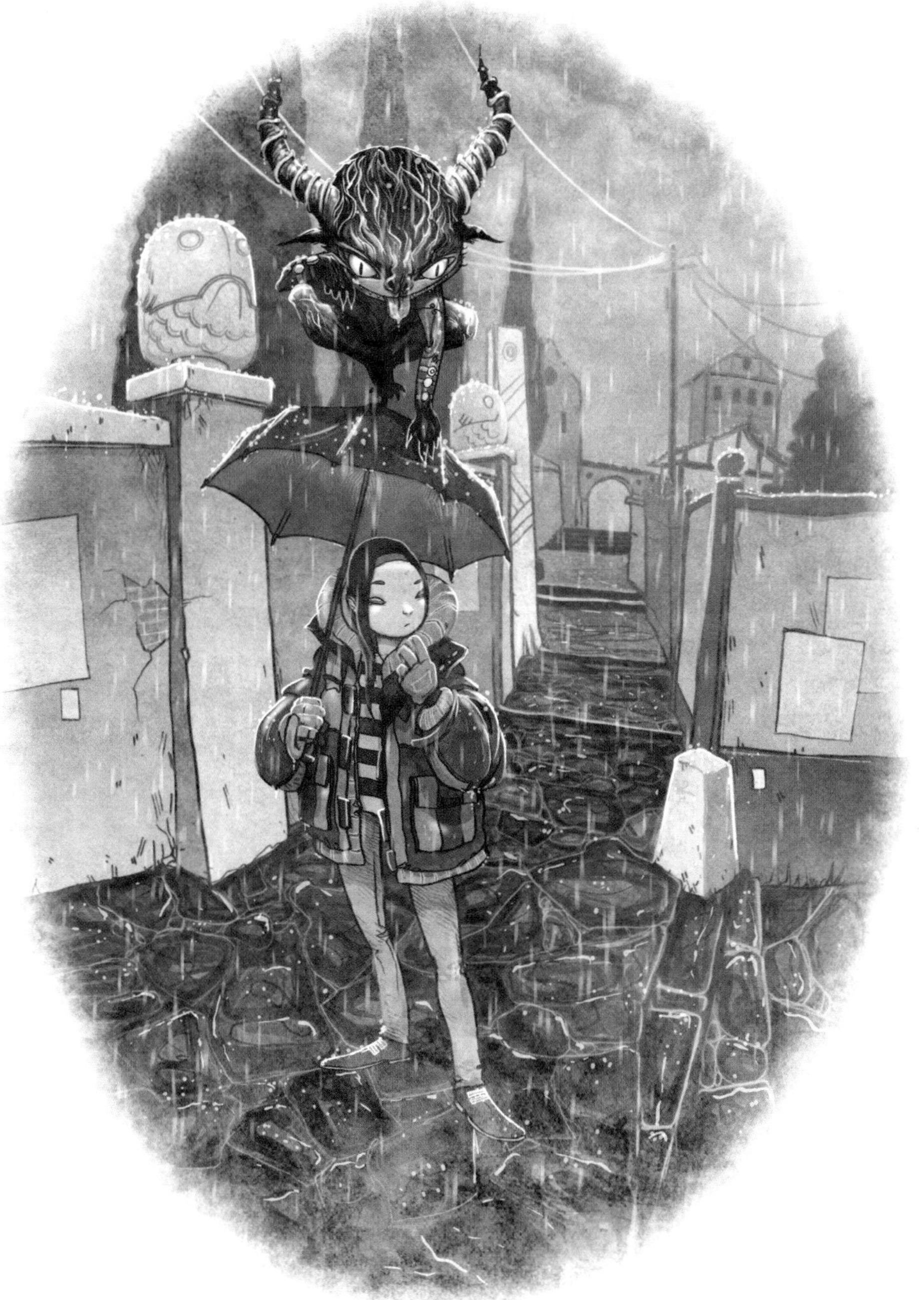

still behind you

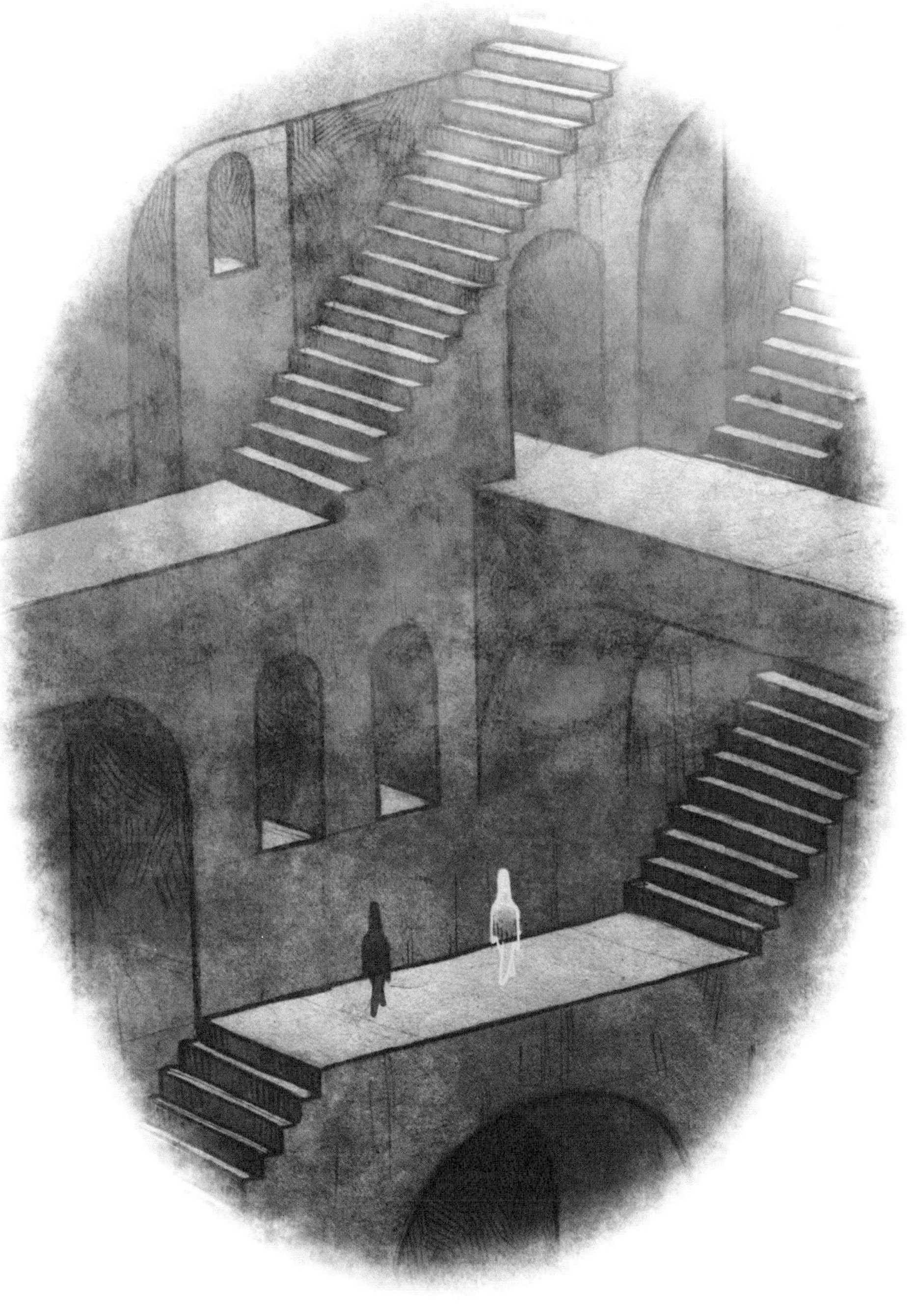

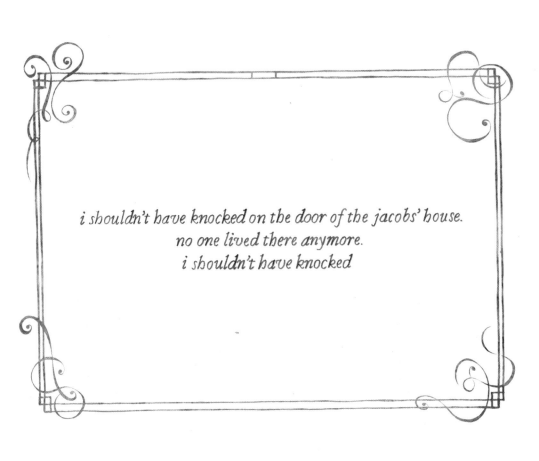

i shouldn't have knocked on the door of the jacobs' house.
no one lived there anymore.
i shouldn't have knocked

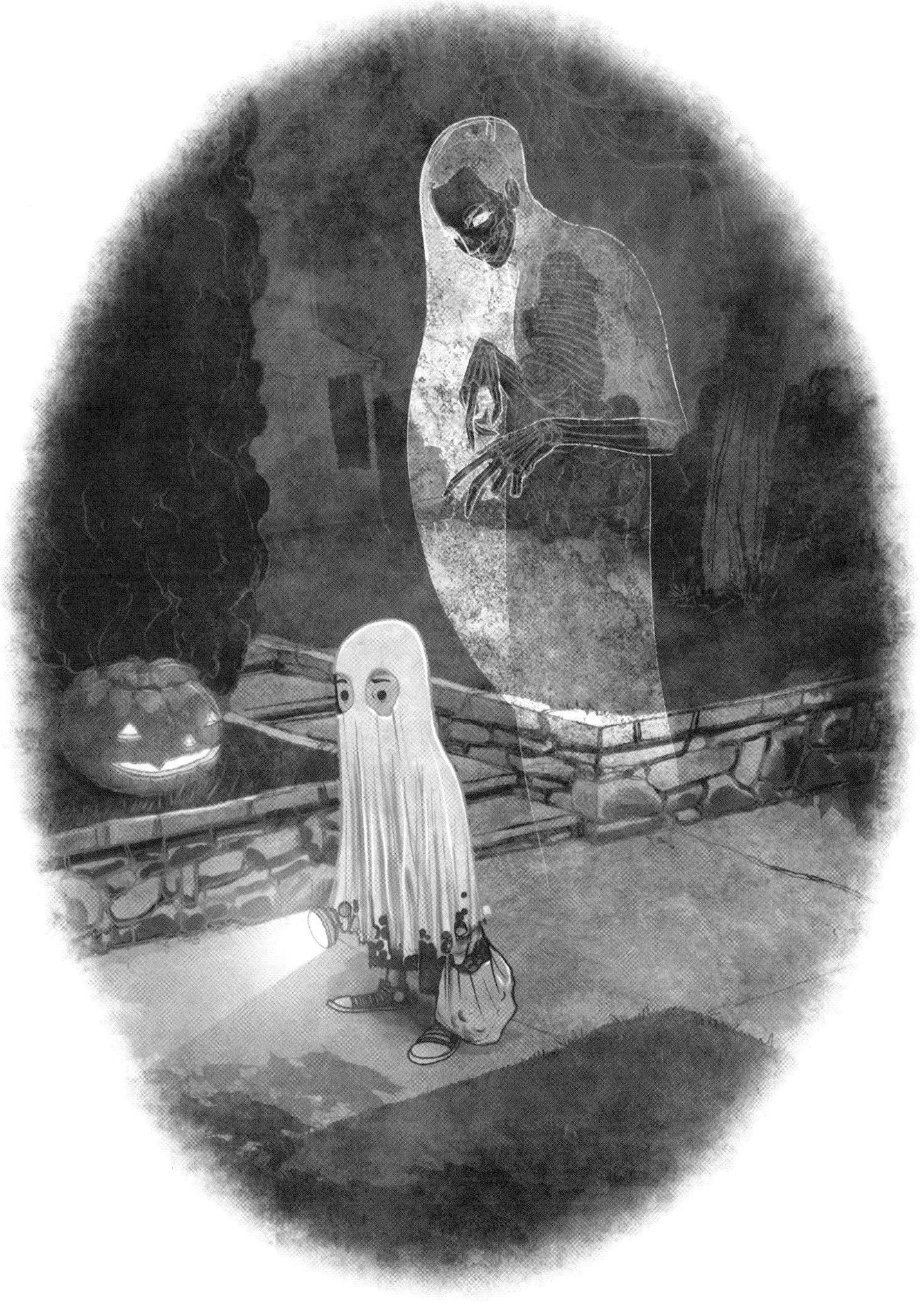

she bought the hat online and borrowed the bag,
the old broom she just found
out on the path through the woods

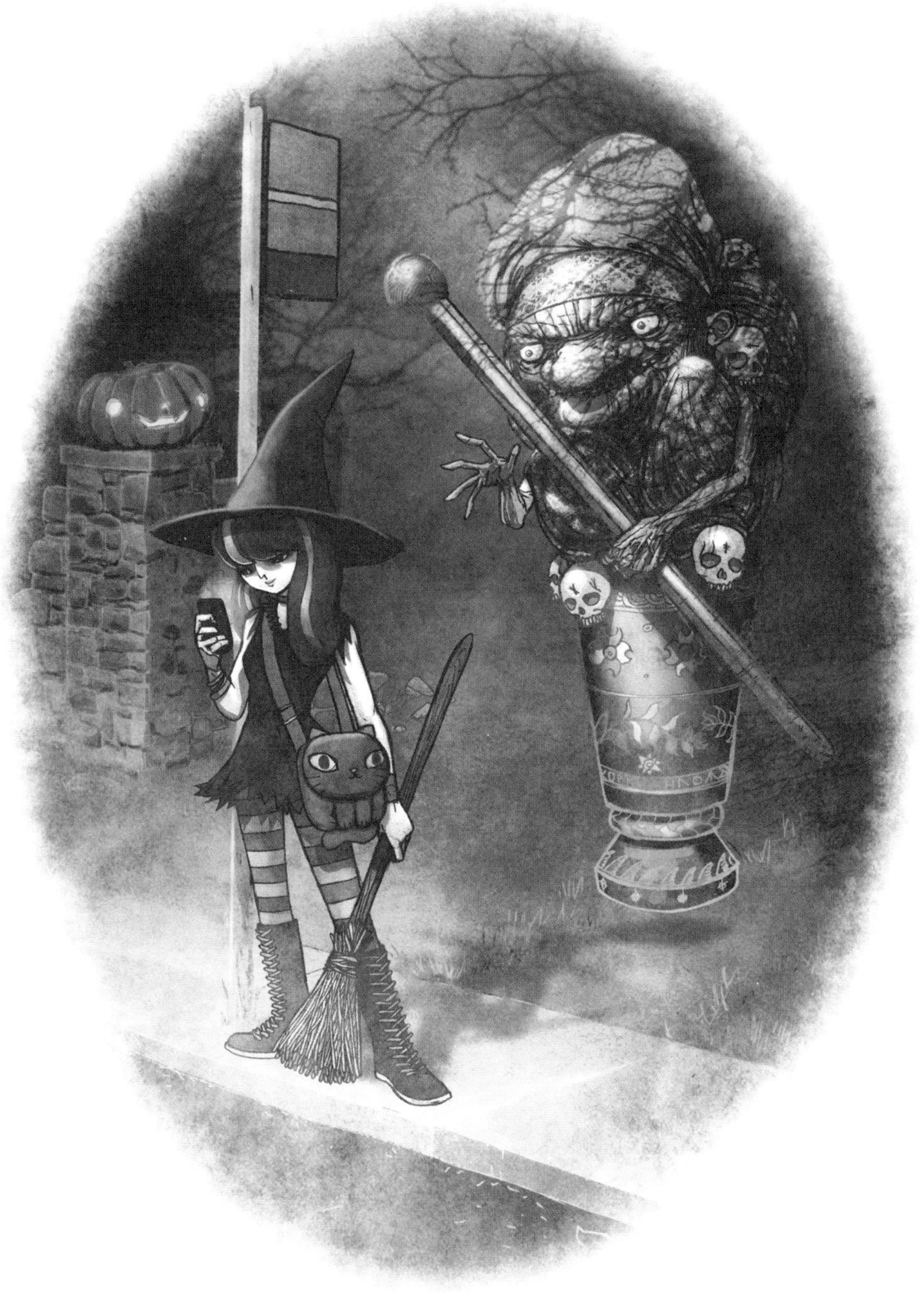

it was a dare.
he could pretend he did it, but he wanted to see.
so he looked in the mirror and said the word three times

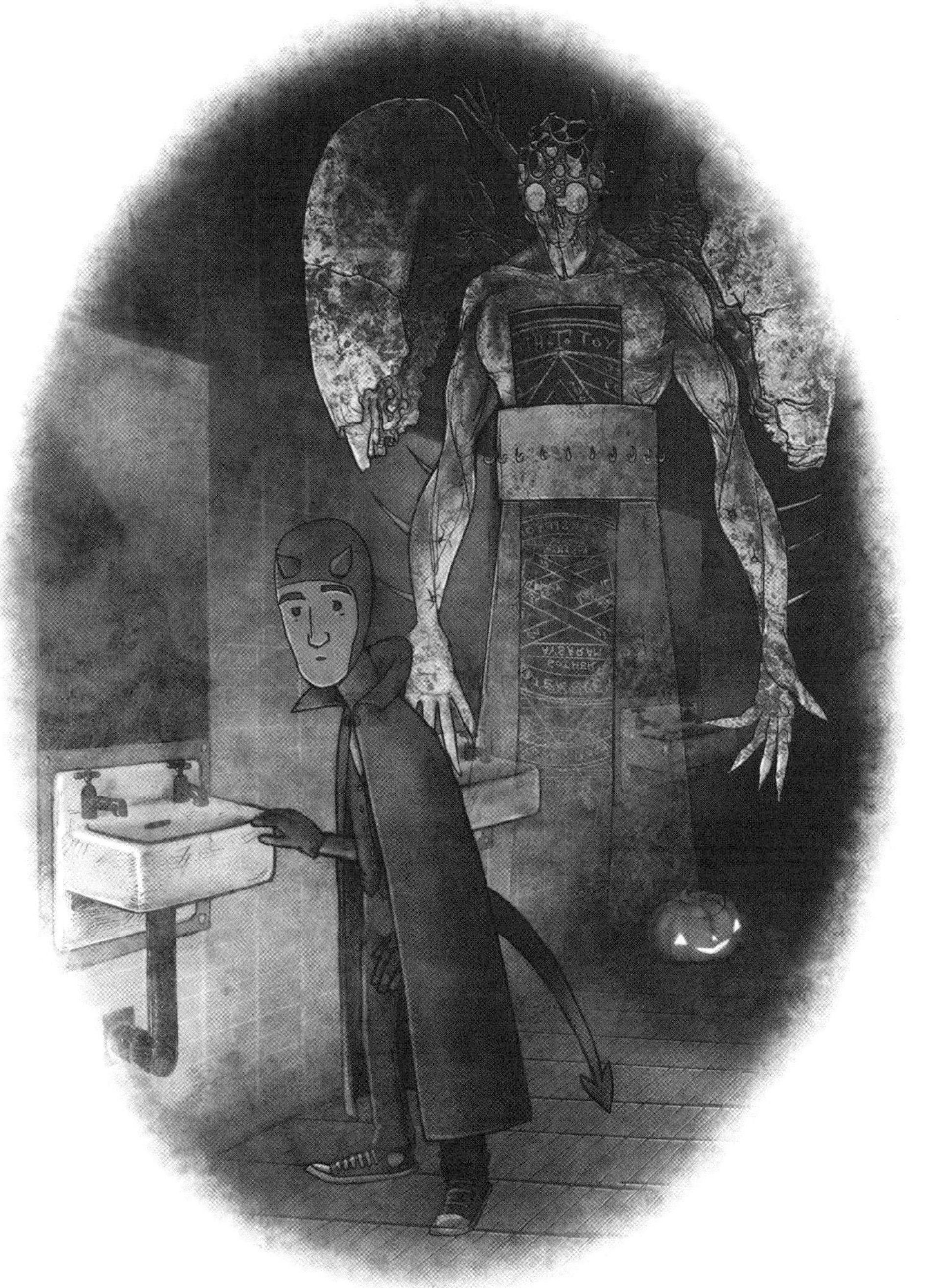

this would be the best halloween party ever.
every kid in the neighbourhood had been invited

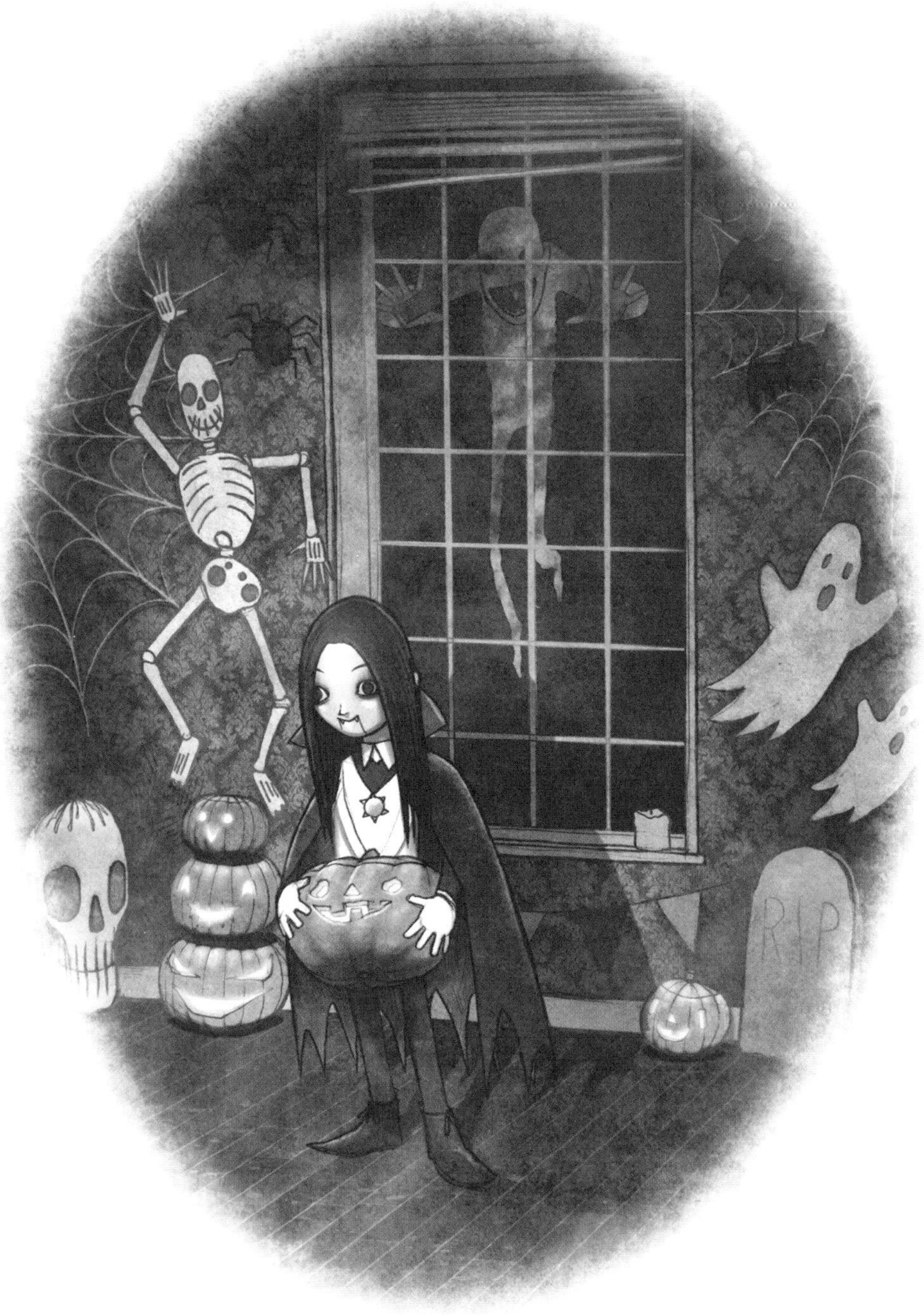
RIP

it was fun as a kid,
but now

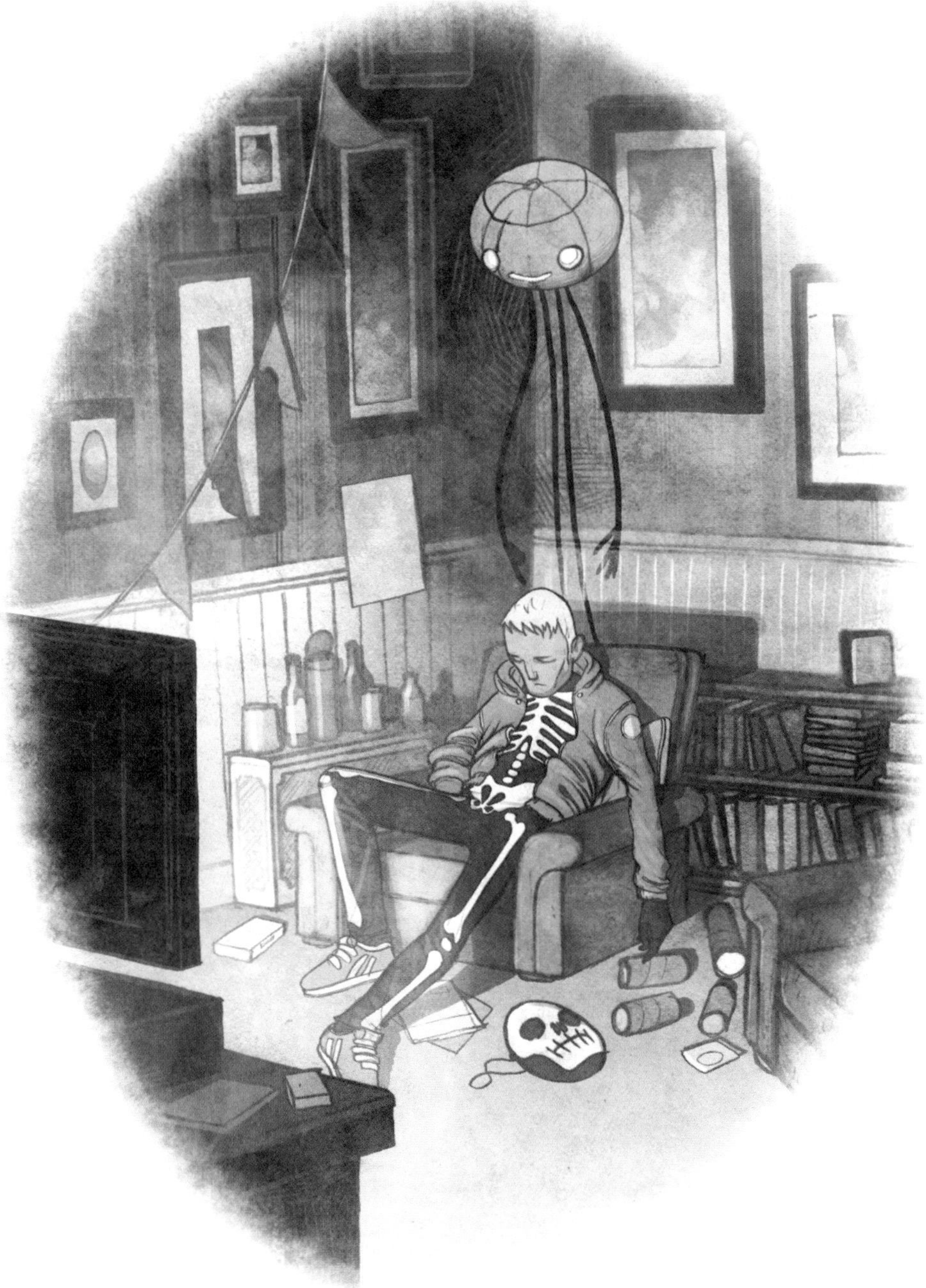

my new friend made strange company.
he never left my side.
after the sun set he began to let out a low whine and stare off

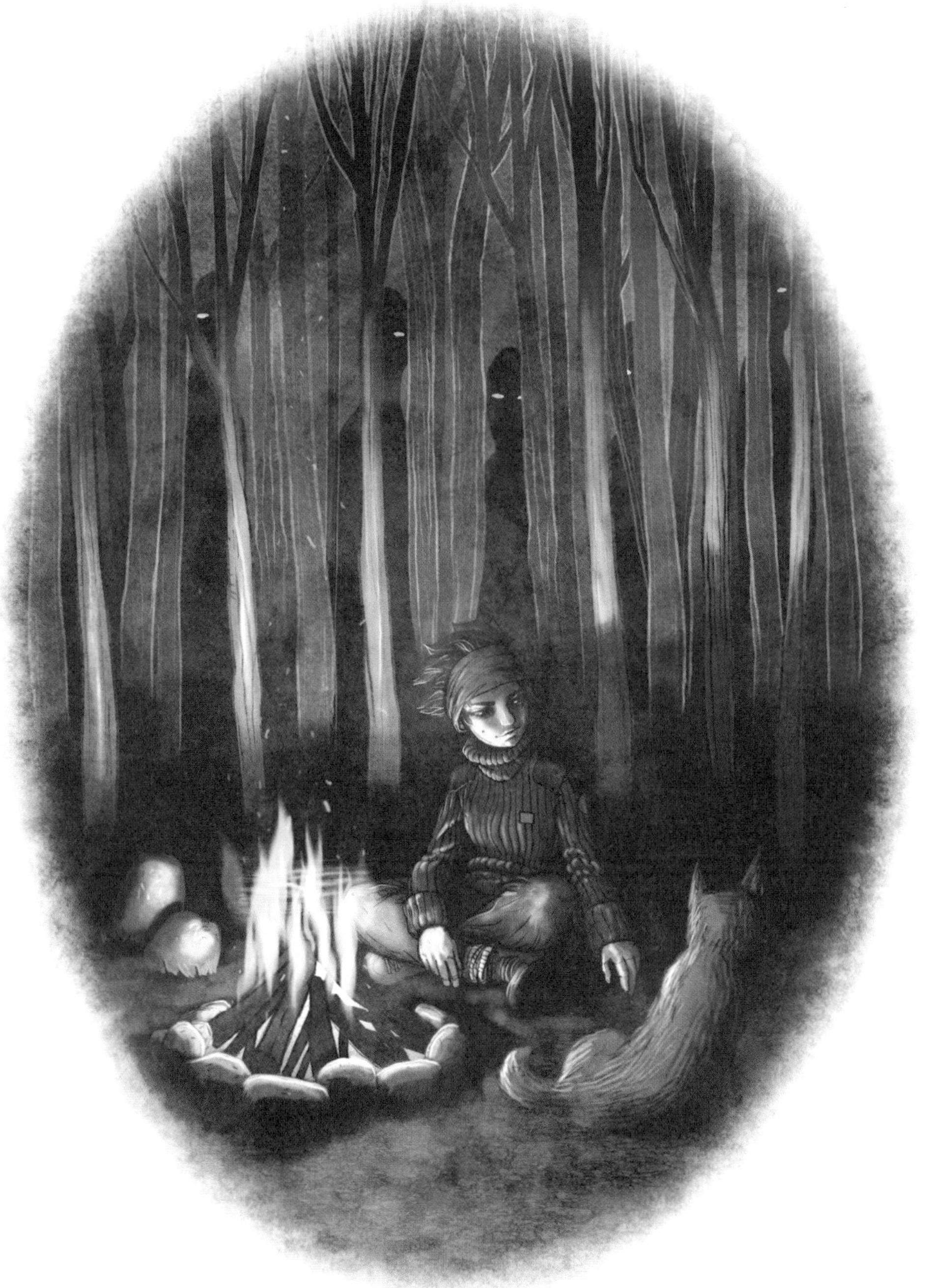

i used to know every corner of this place by heart.
now i have it half forgotten

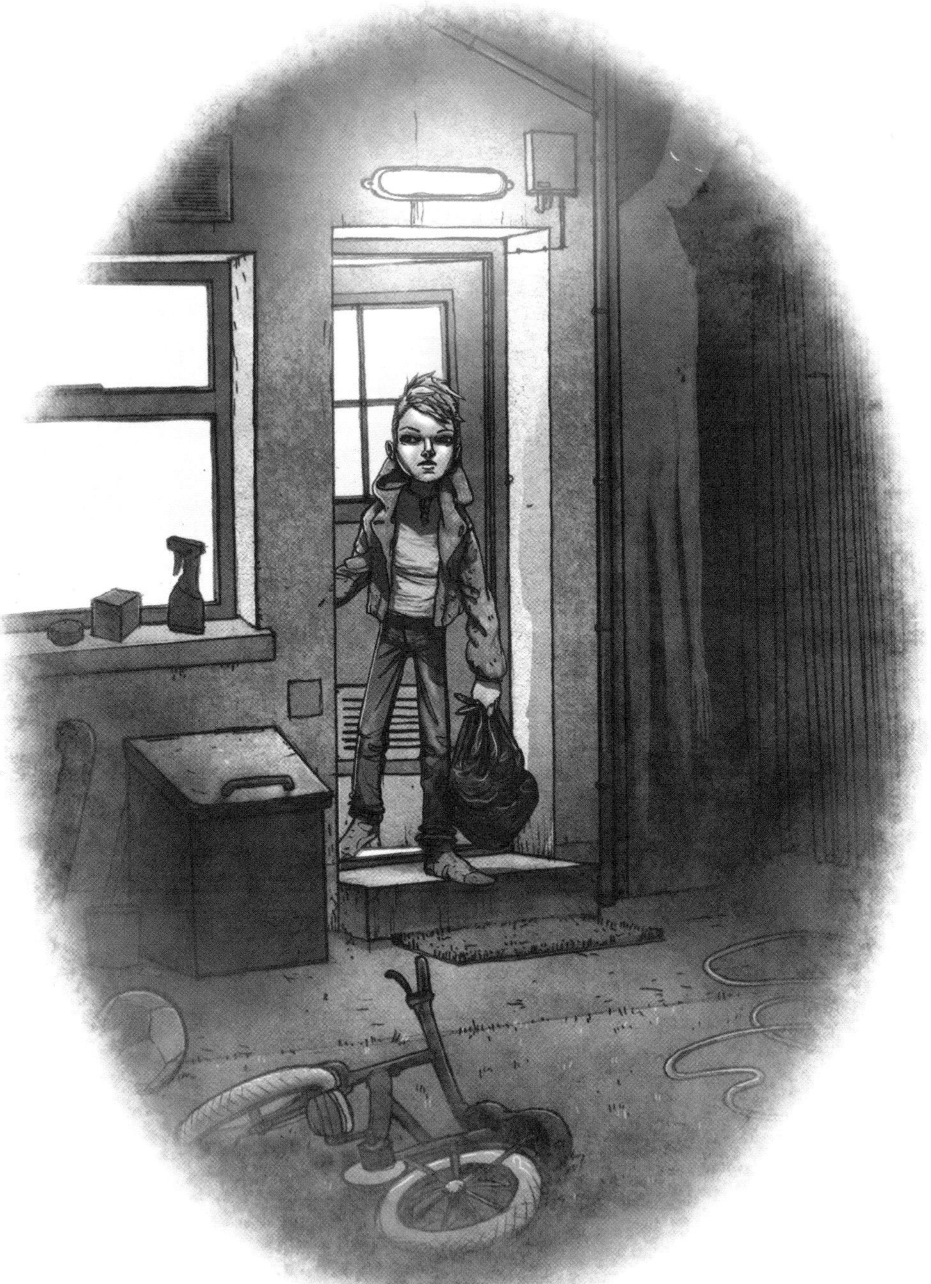

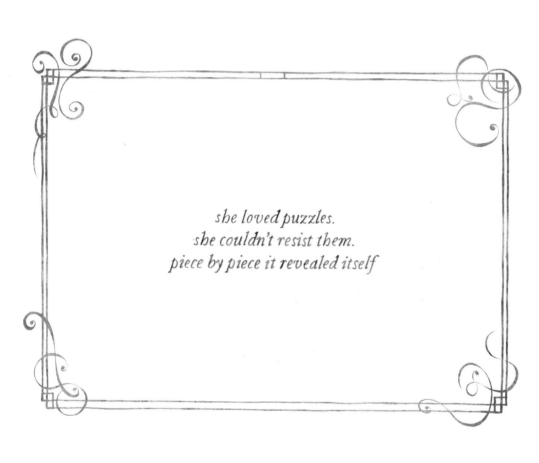

she loved puzzles.
she couldn't resist them.
piece by piece it revealed itself

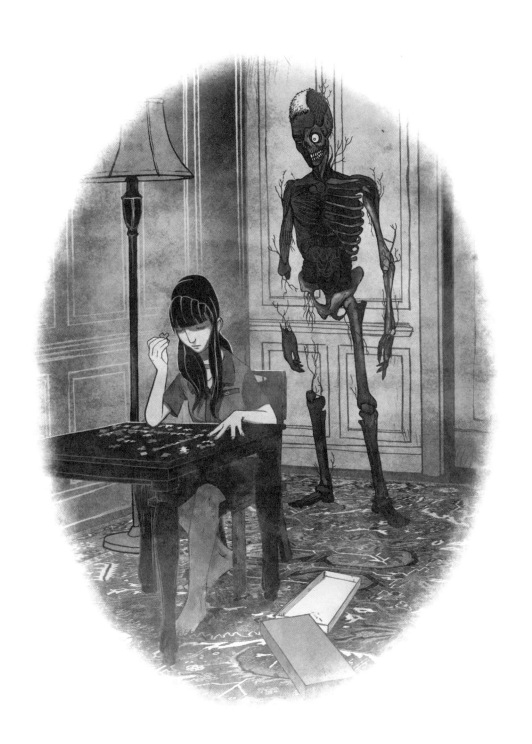

must have been something here once.
gone now

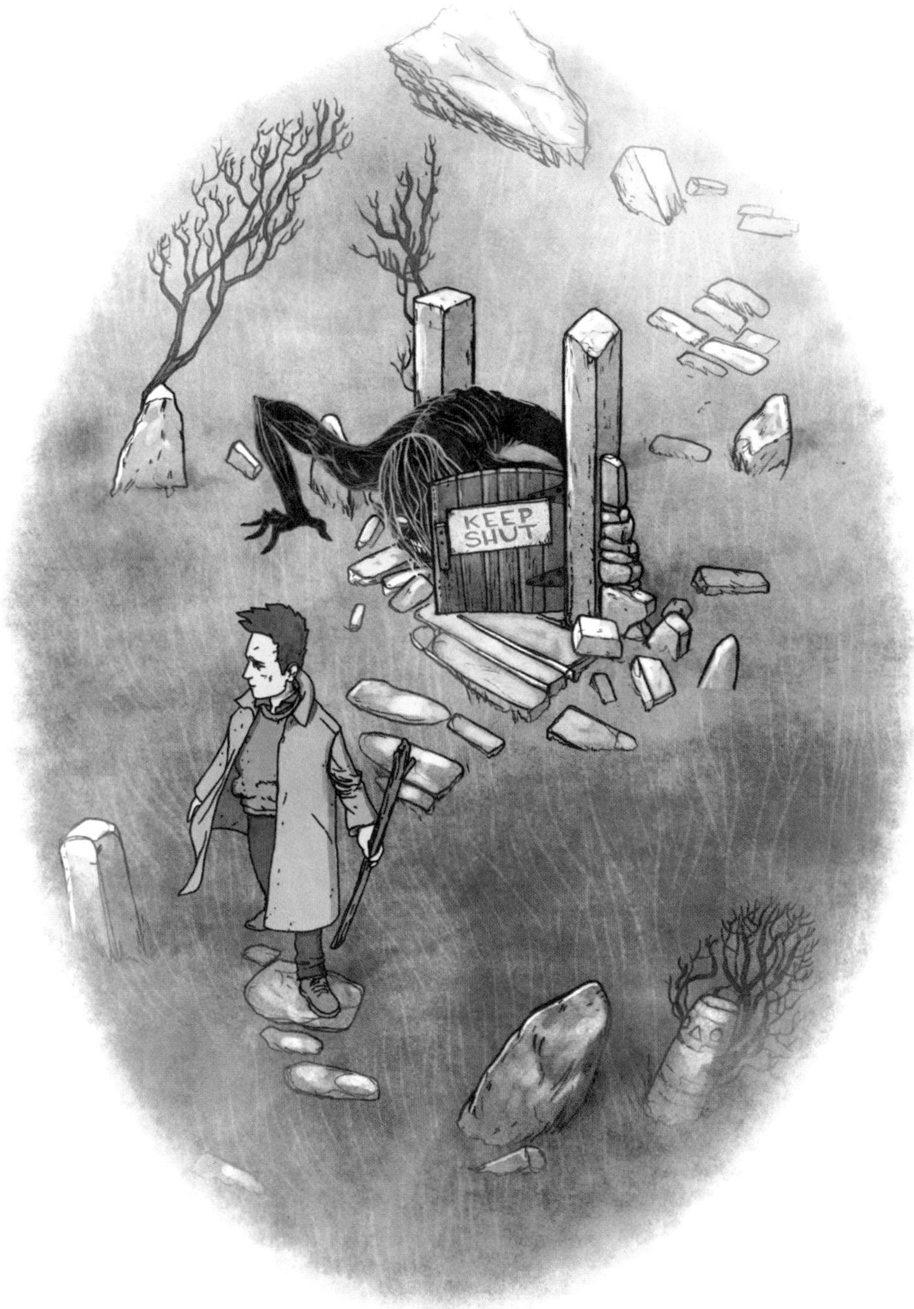
KEEP
SHUT

this. is. gross.
and worse:
there is definitely someone else in here

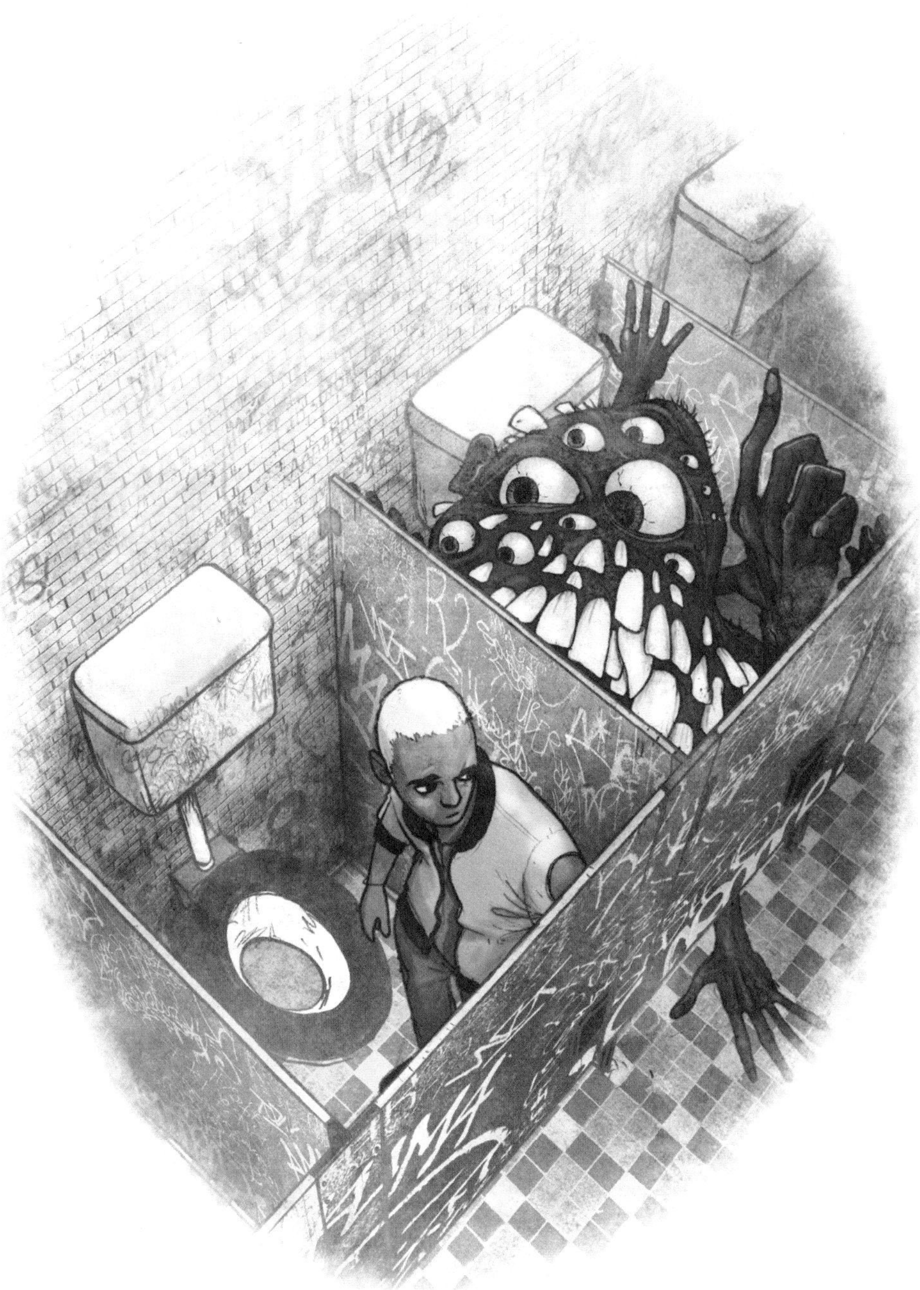

it was stupid to come out over the flooded town.
there's never any fish.
the waters are just bad luck

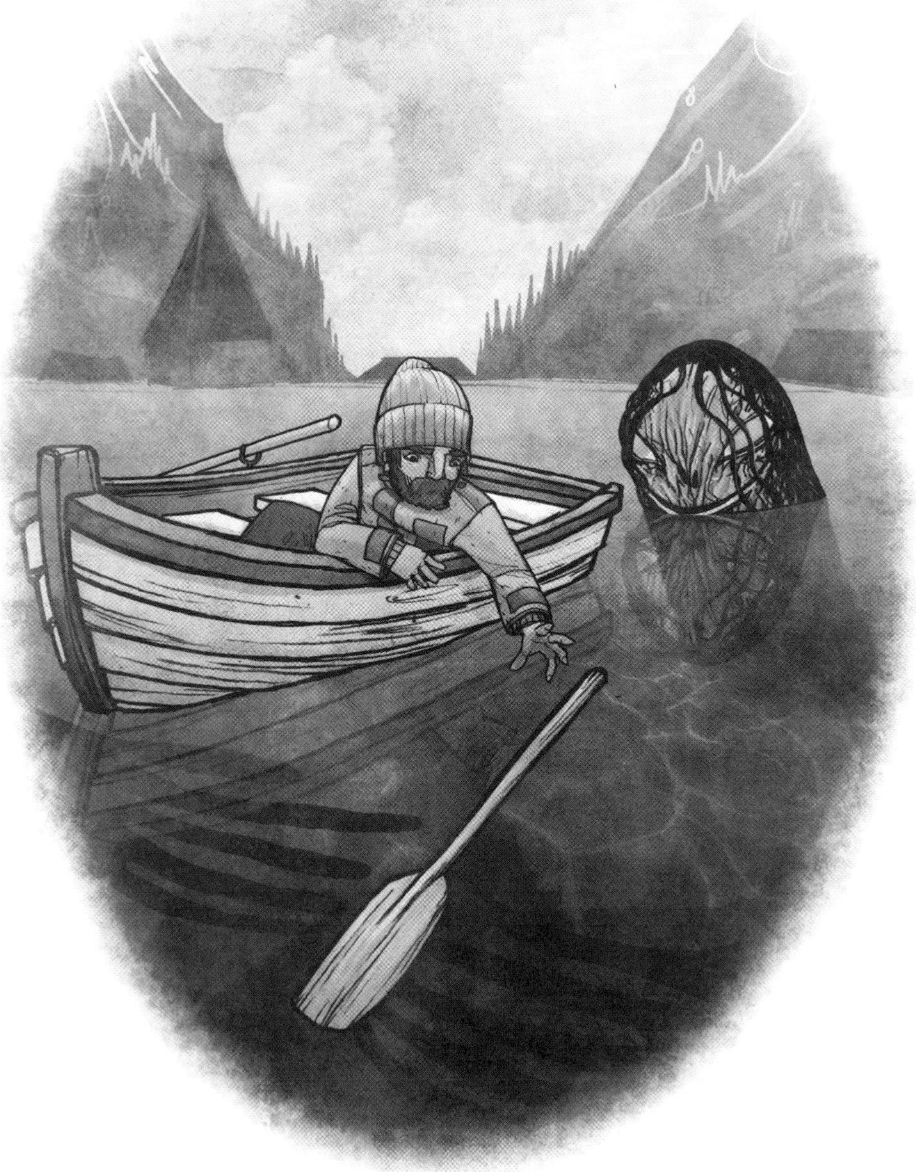

wasn't this where I came in?
how do you get out of this place?

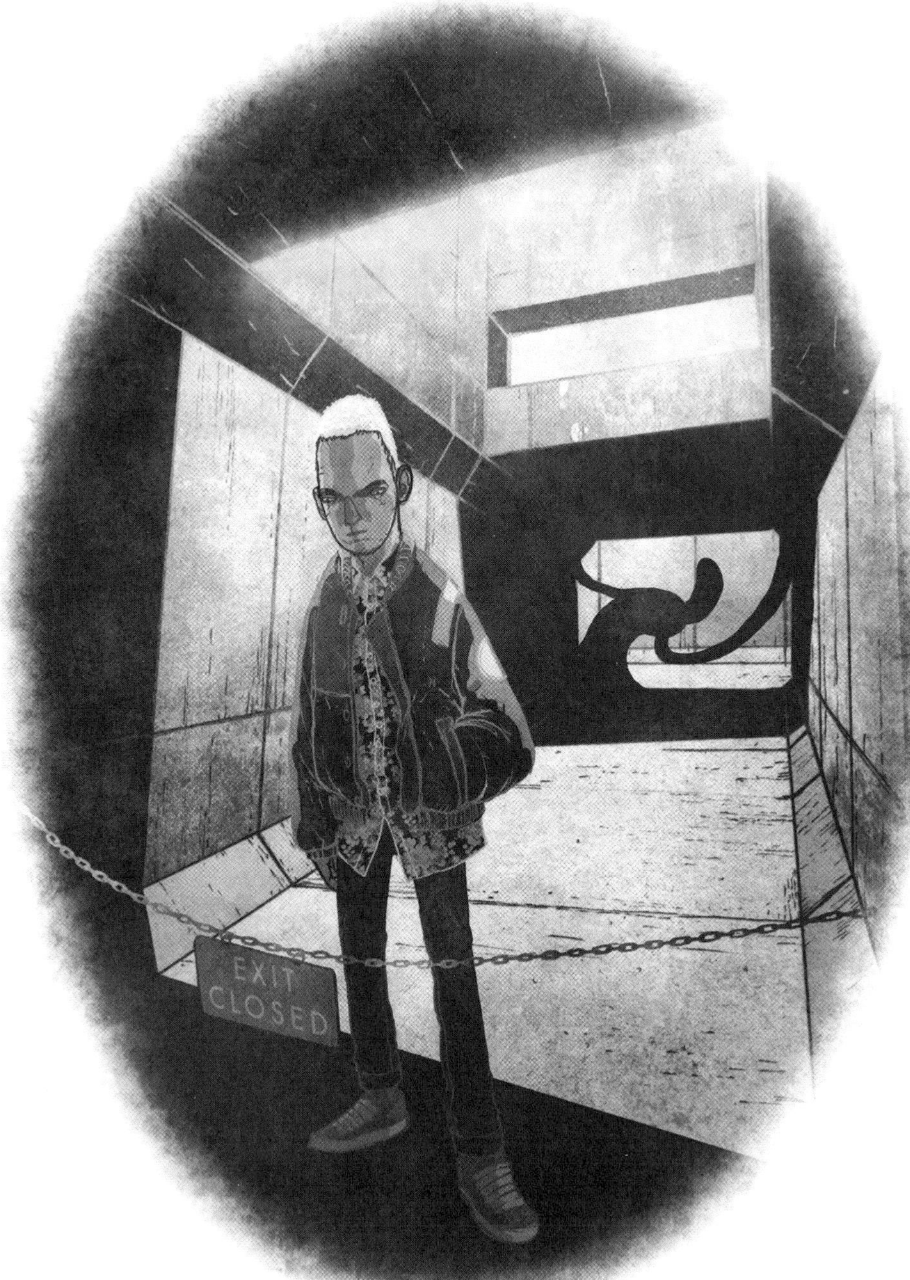
EXIT
CLOSED

when everyone else was fast asleep,
he crept downstairs to wait by the tree,
hoping to catch the man himself

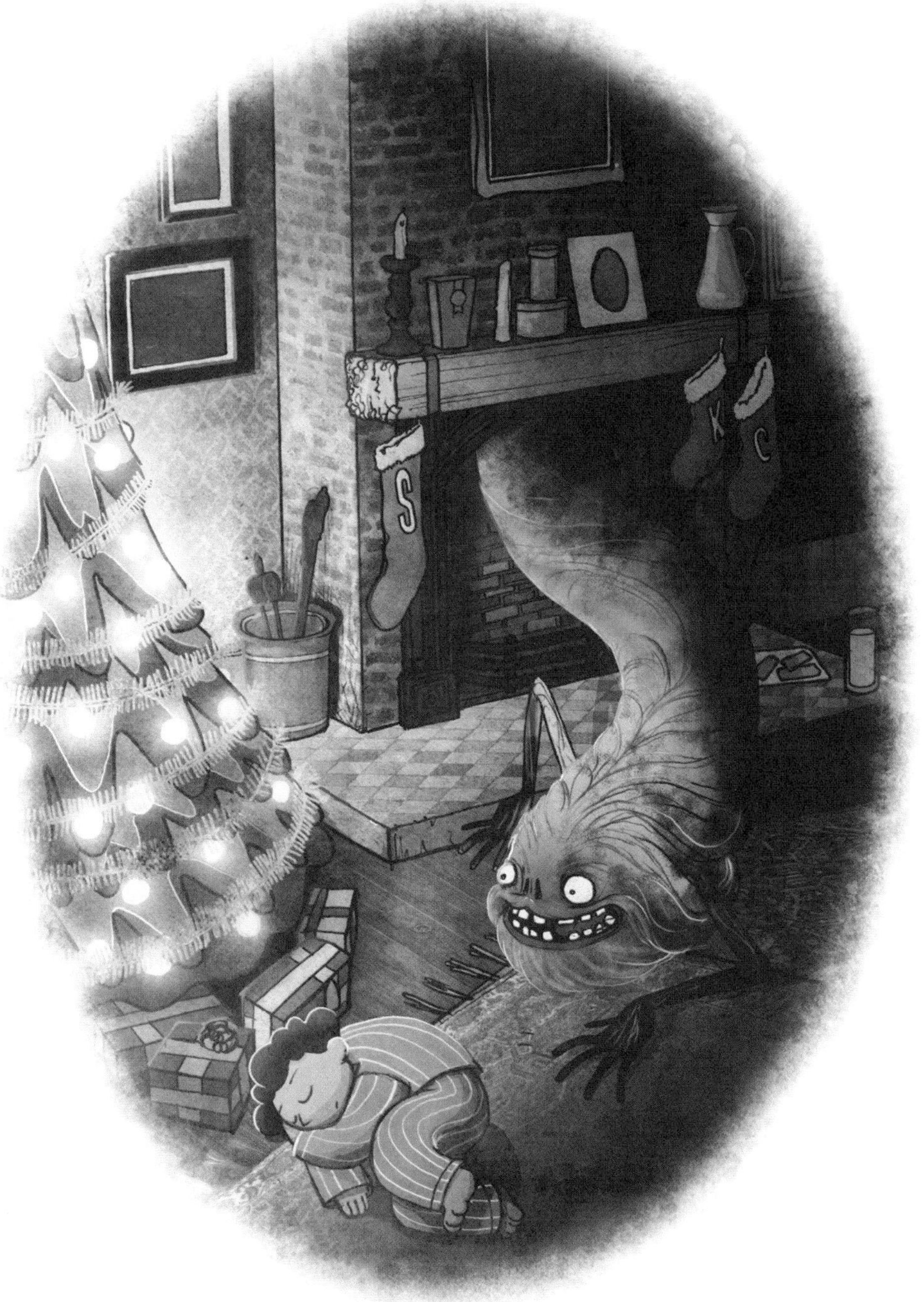
S
K
C

if he failed, he would fail alone
but if he succeeded,
he would succeed with himself for company

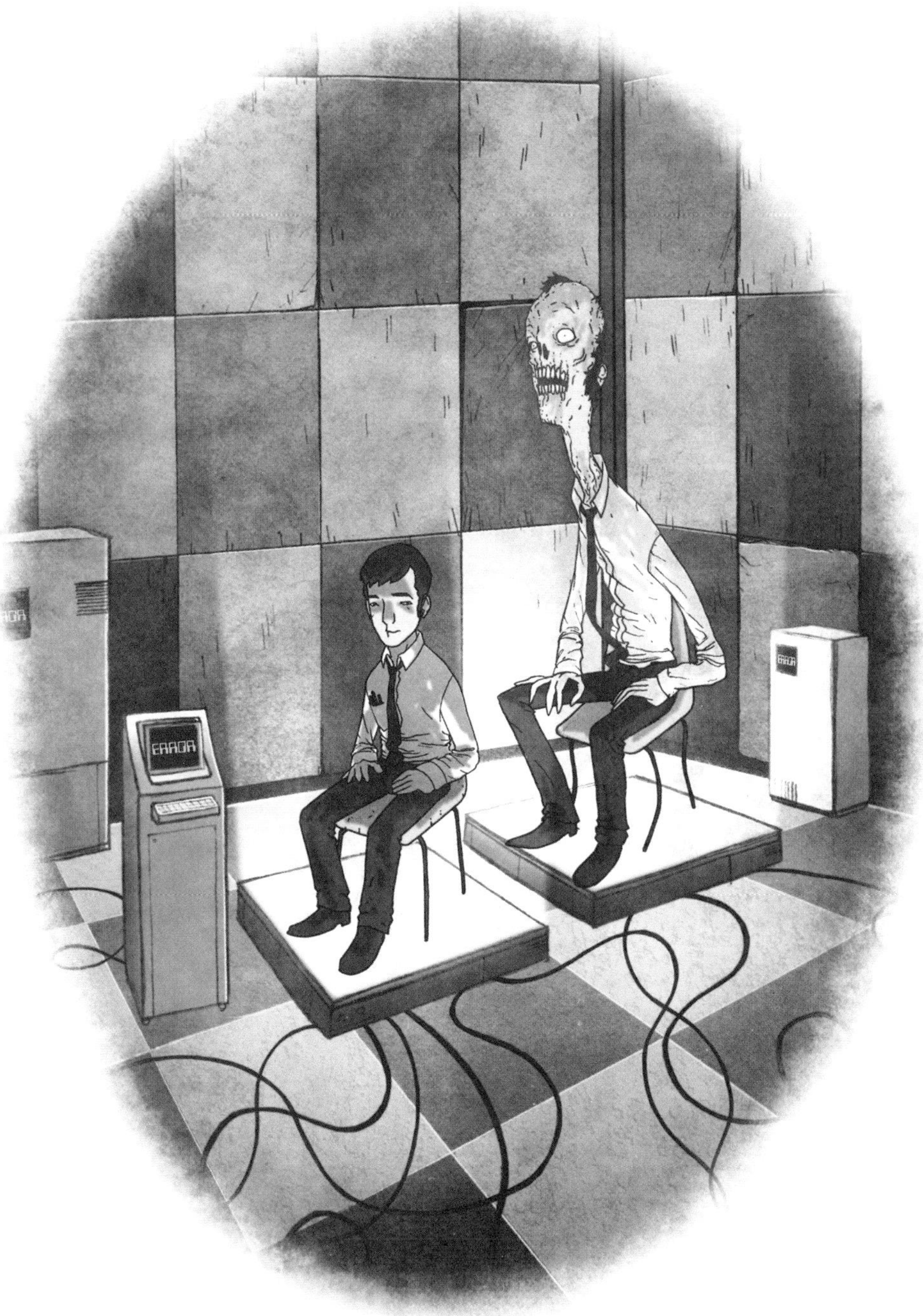
ERROR
ERROR
ERROR

he thought he might have the whole place to himself.
but then he heard the laughter.
one voice? two? more?

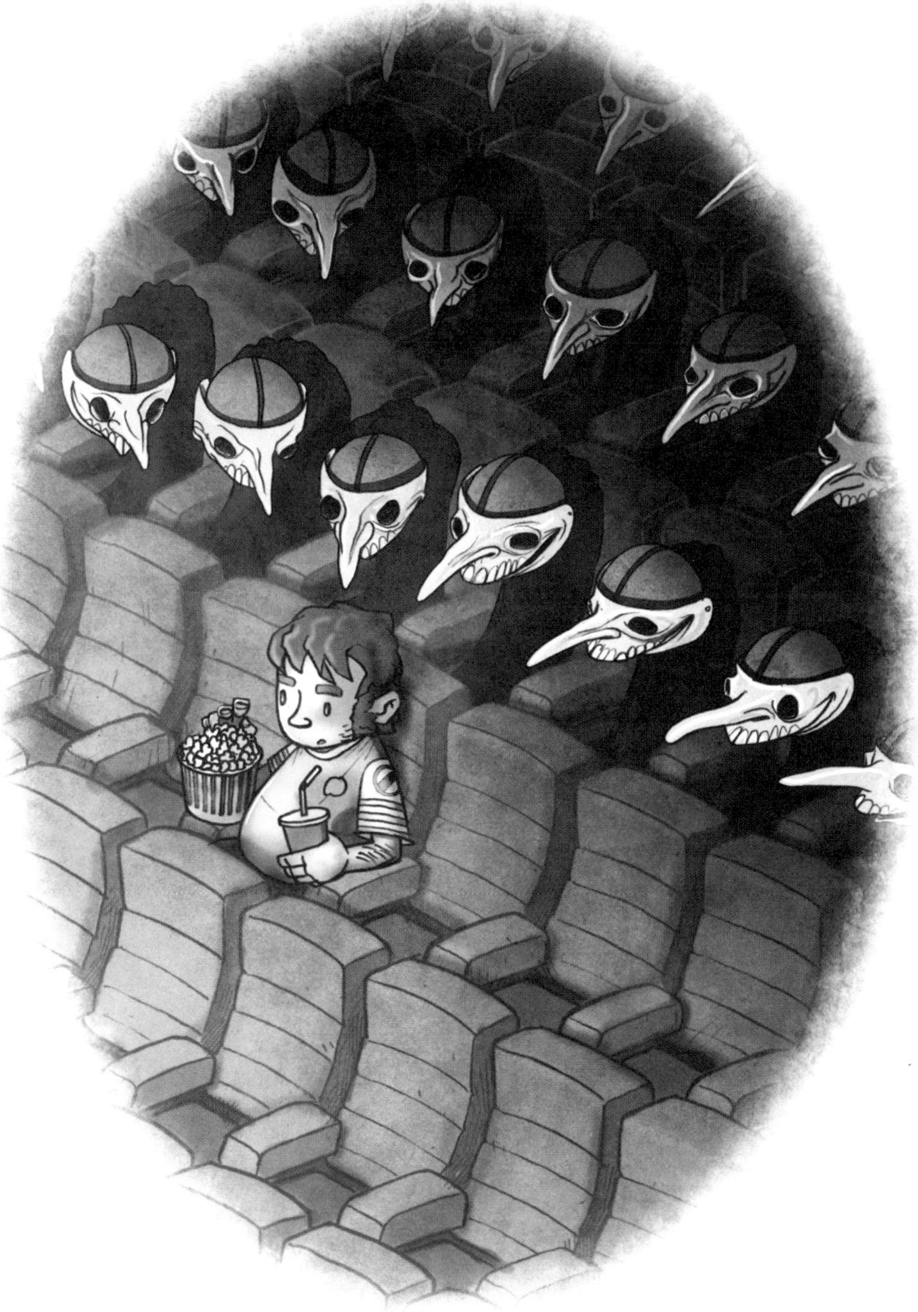

mothers didn't let their kids come here anymore.
no one came here.
it was the perfect place to be alone

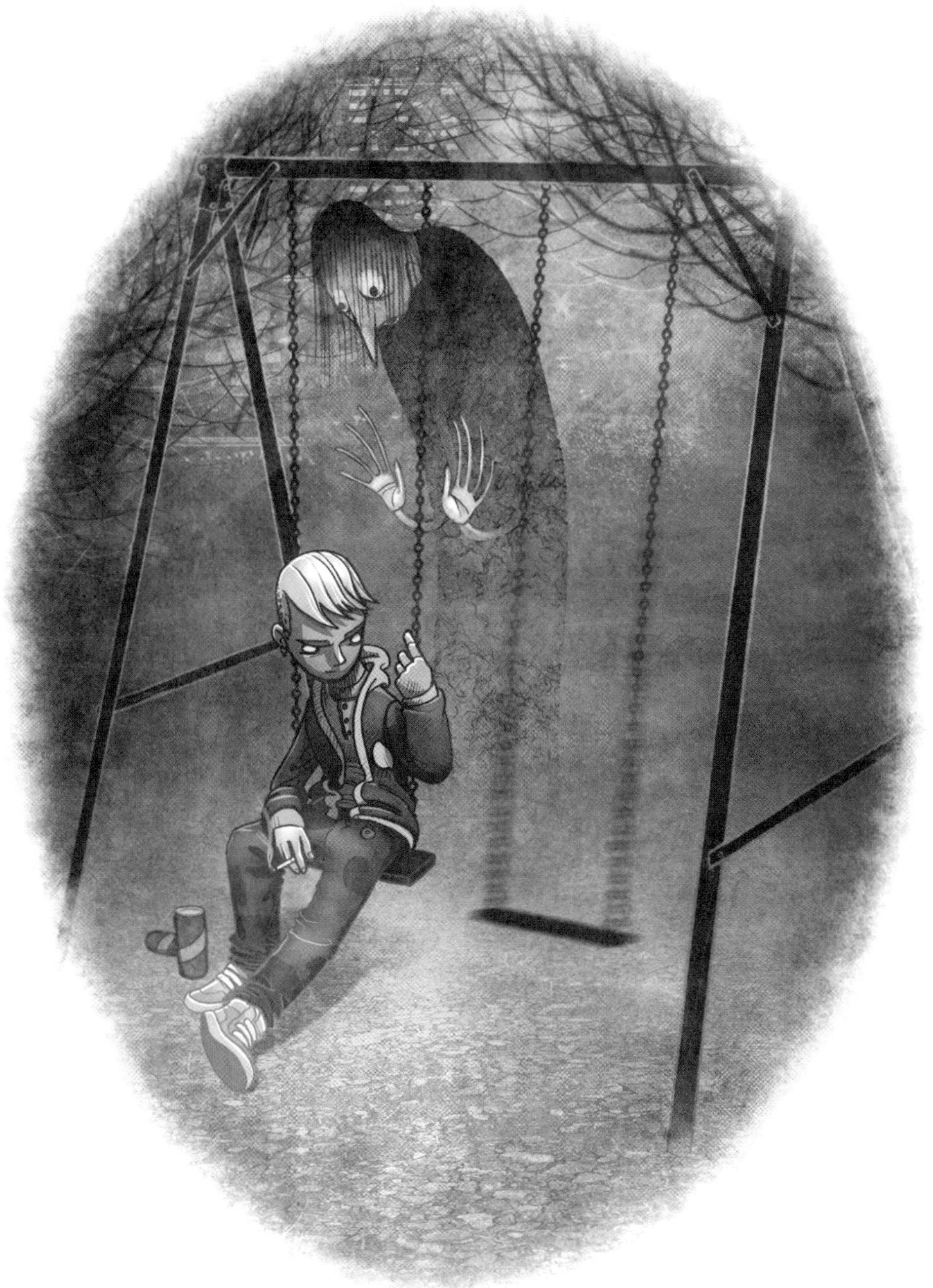

... ninety-six,
ninety-seven,
ninety-eight,
ninety-nine...

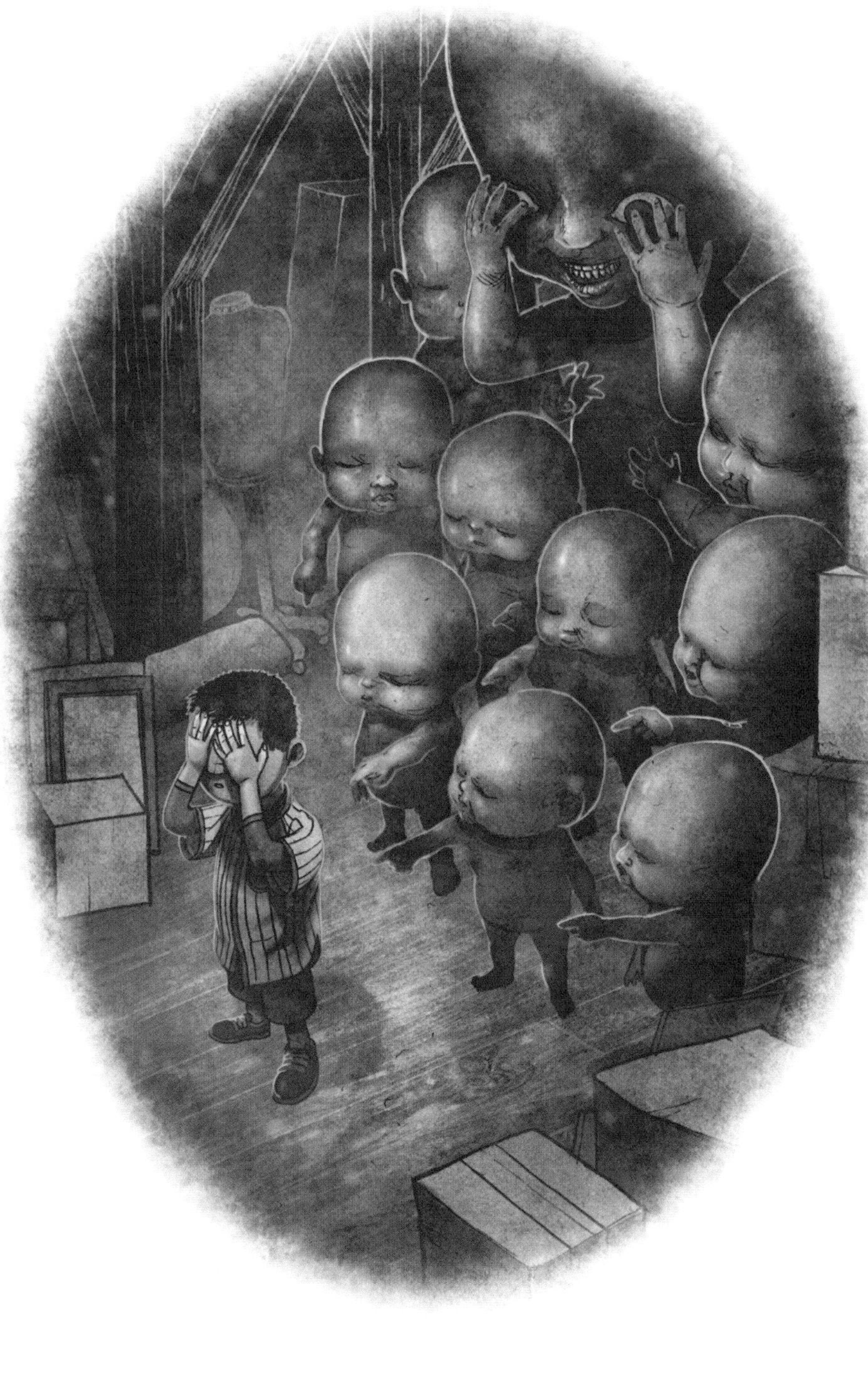

hungry, so hungry.
starving.
up in the middle of the night to find something to eat

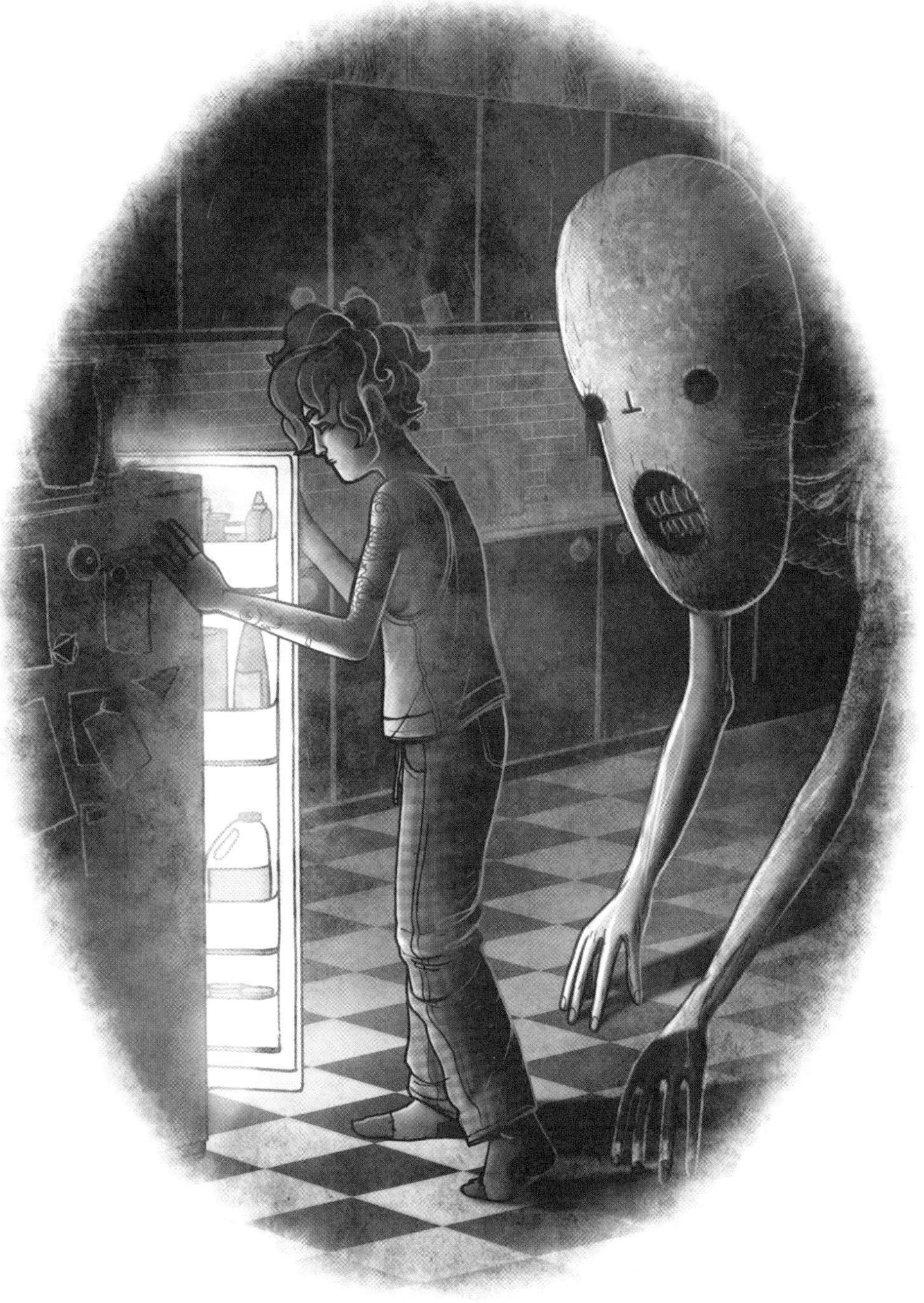

it had the highest walls and the toughest locks,
but the house's contents looked worth his efforts

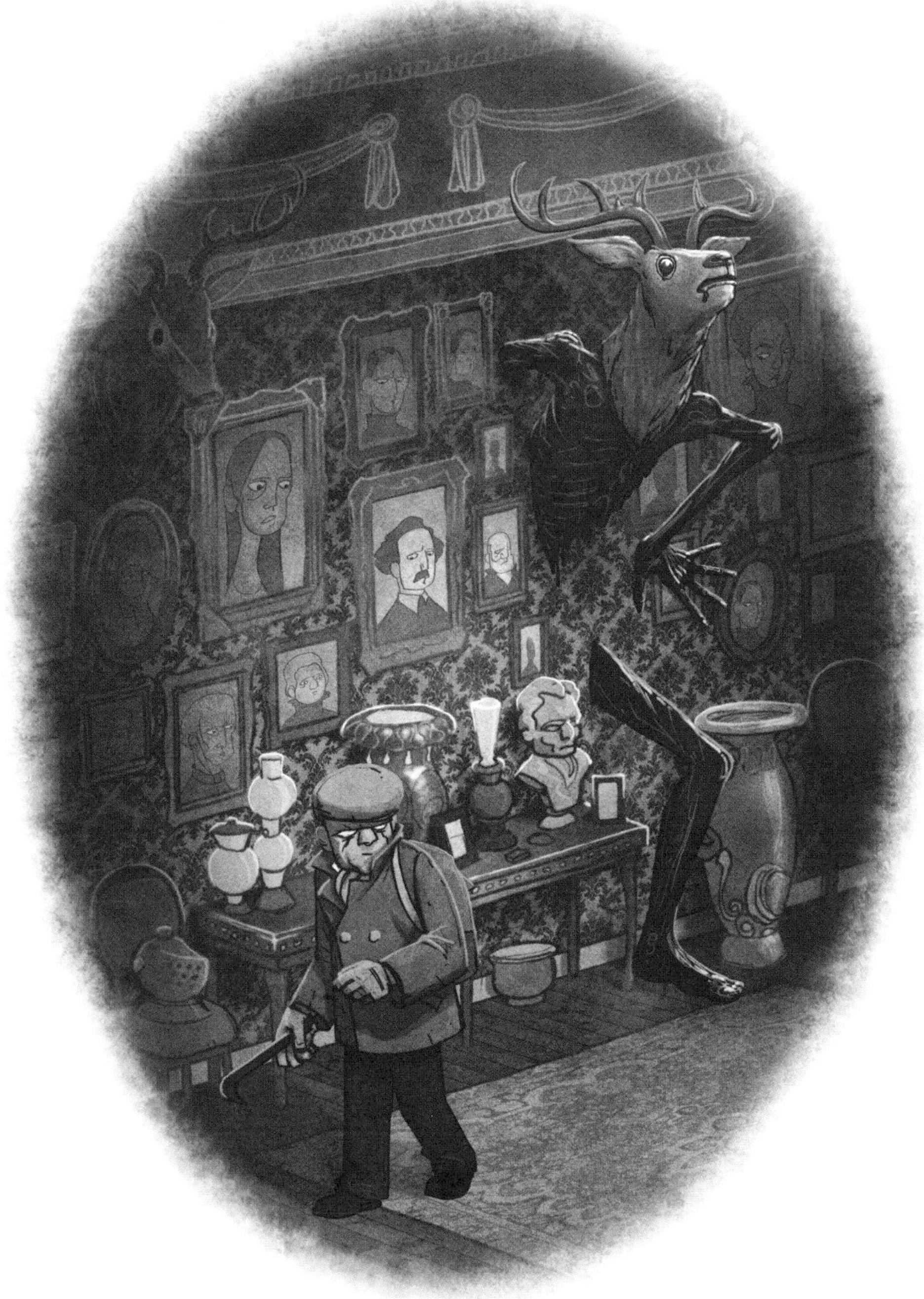

a door in his mind swung open
and his soul wandered out to explore new tiers,
leaving his empty shell behind him

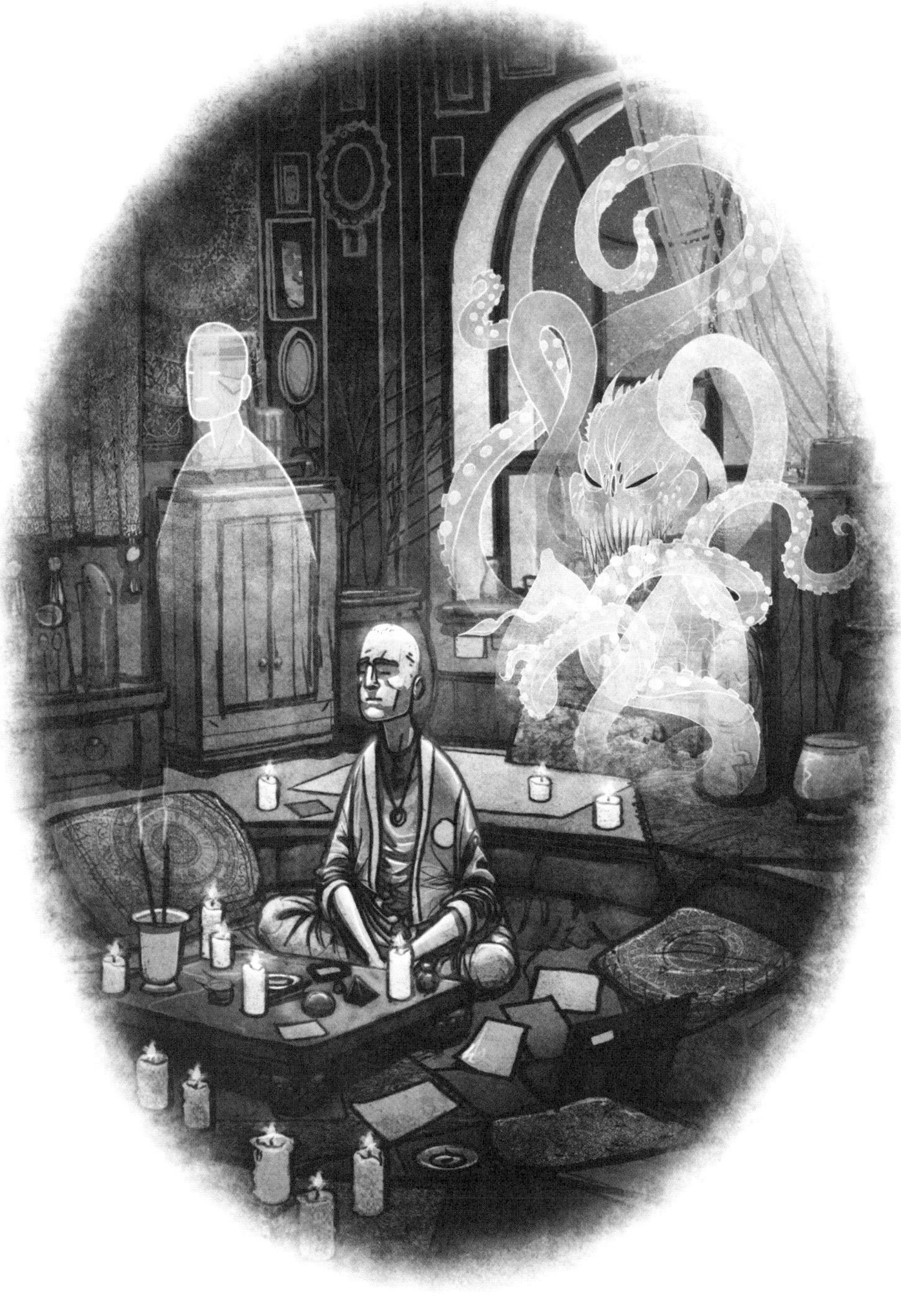

as the only brother left,
the house was finally his.
but it didn't feel the same place now its rooms were empty

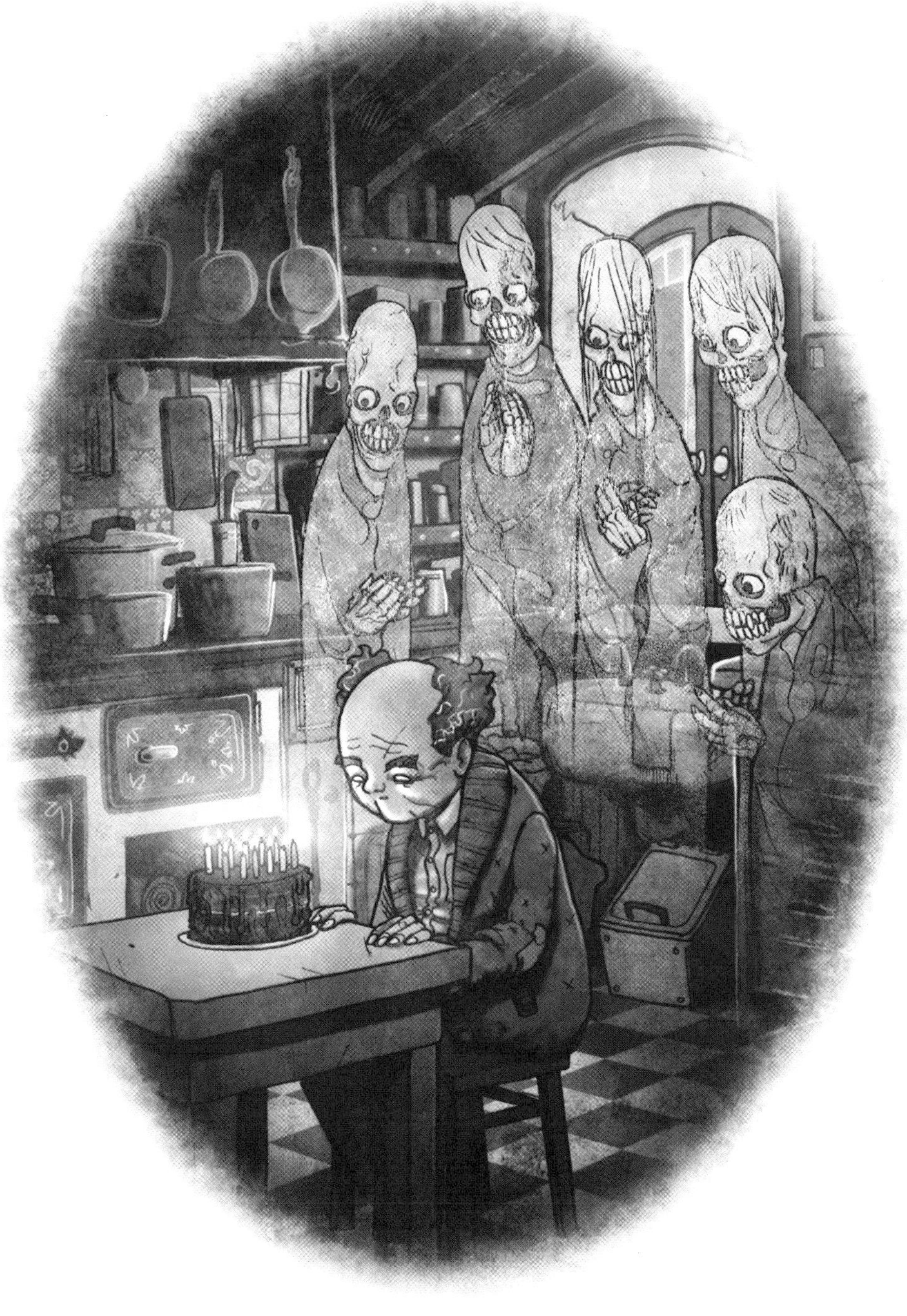

everyone had gone home but there was still more to be done.
if anyone else took the work seriously he wouldn't be alone

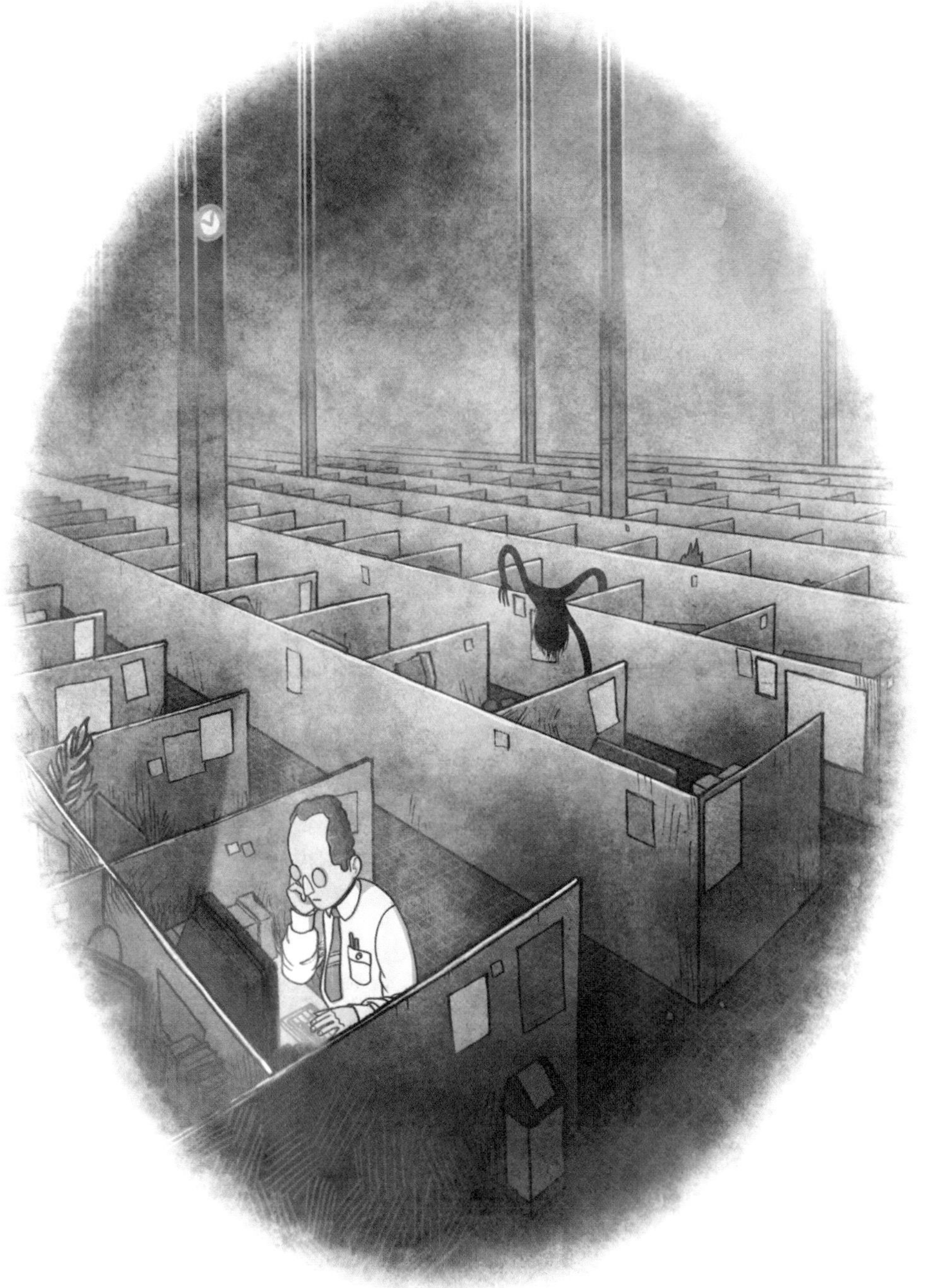

from here you could watch them go by

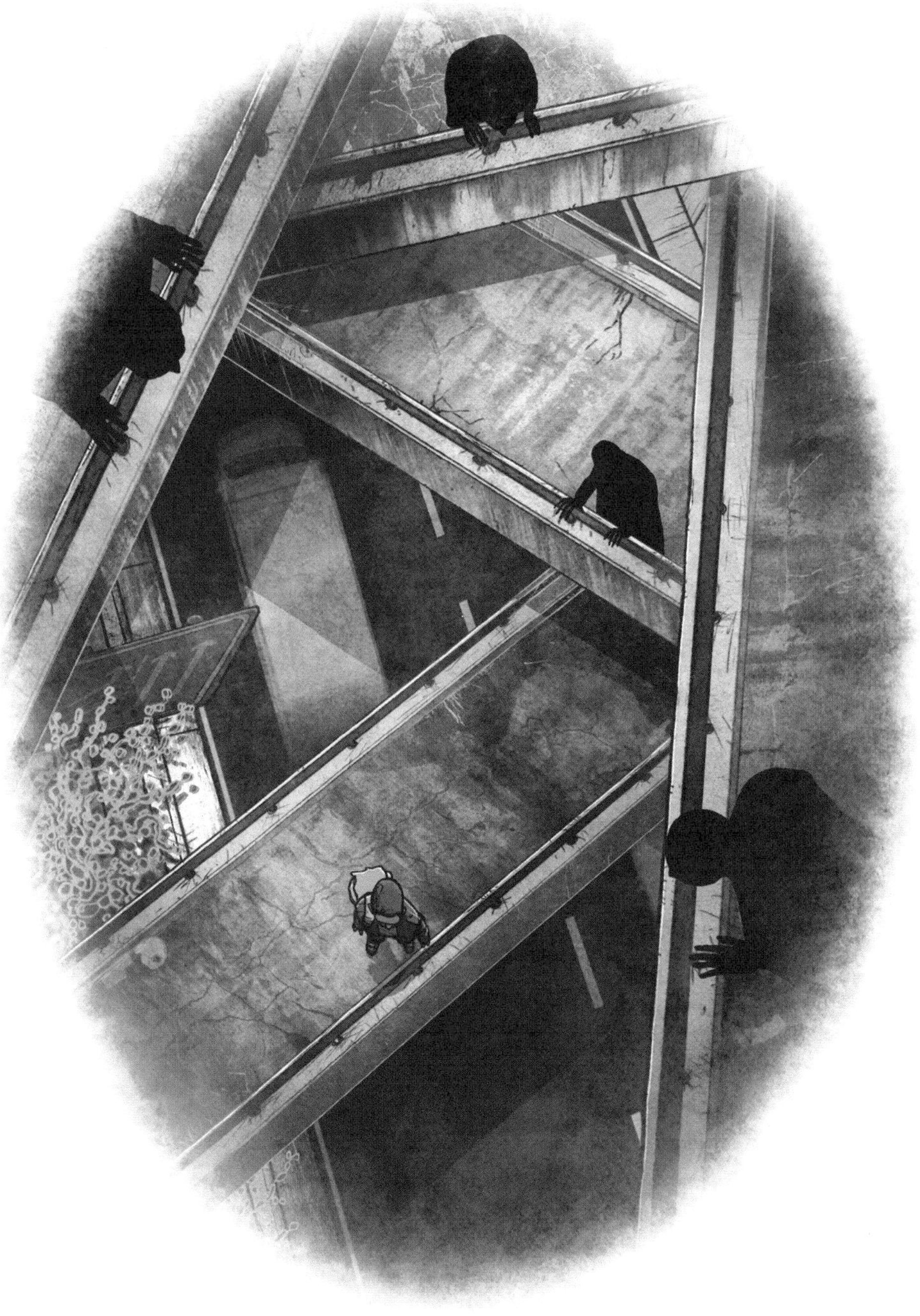

let them go on the stupid ghost train if they want.
i'd had enough.
i hate the circus

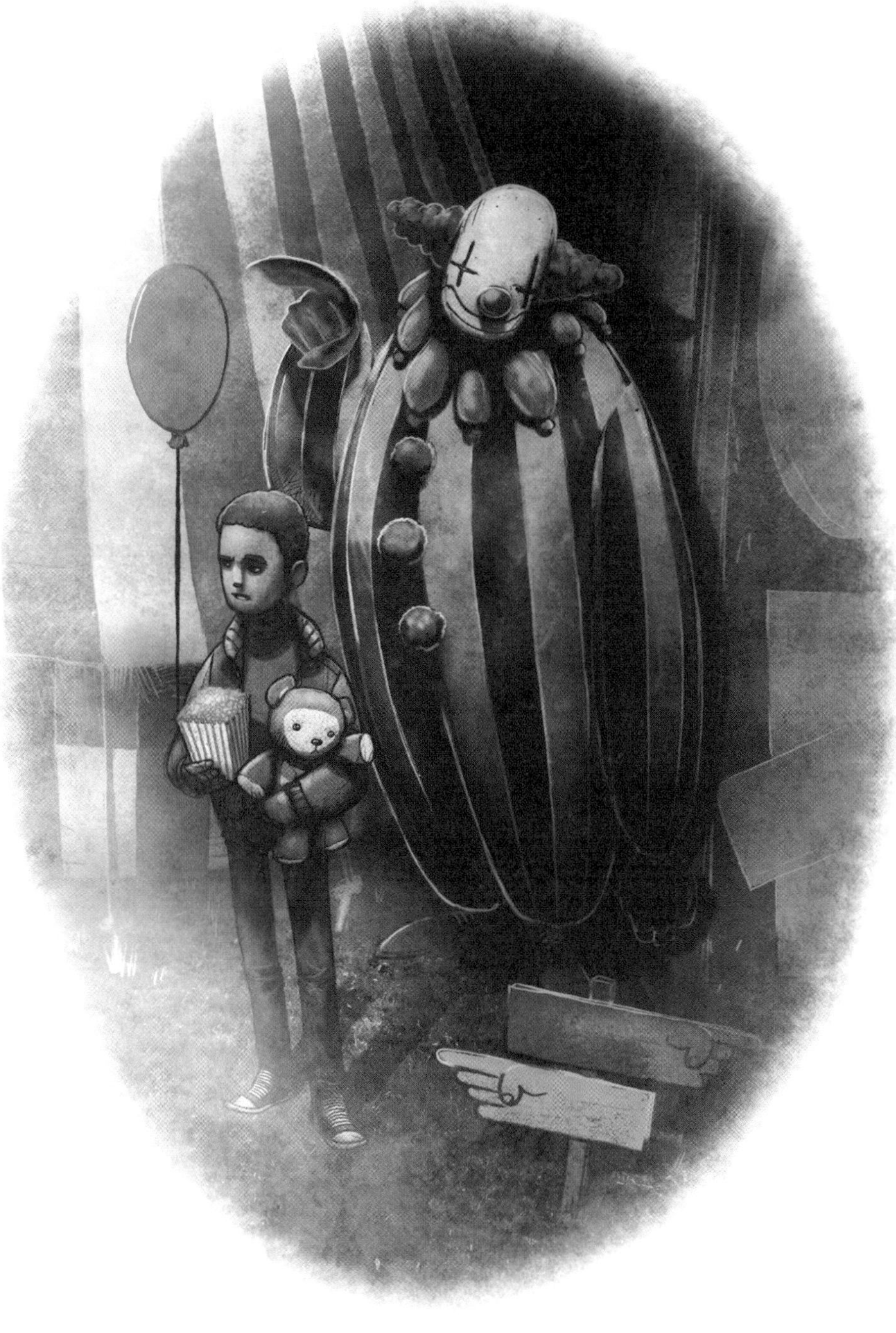

he had never seen any of the locals use the bridge,
but tonight he found it unlocked
and couldn't resist crossing it

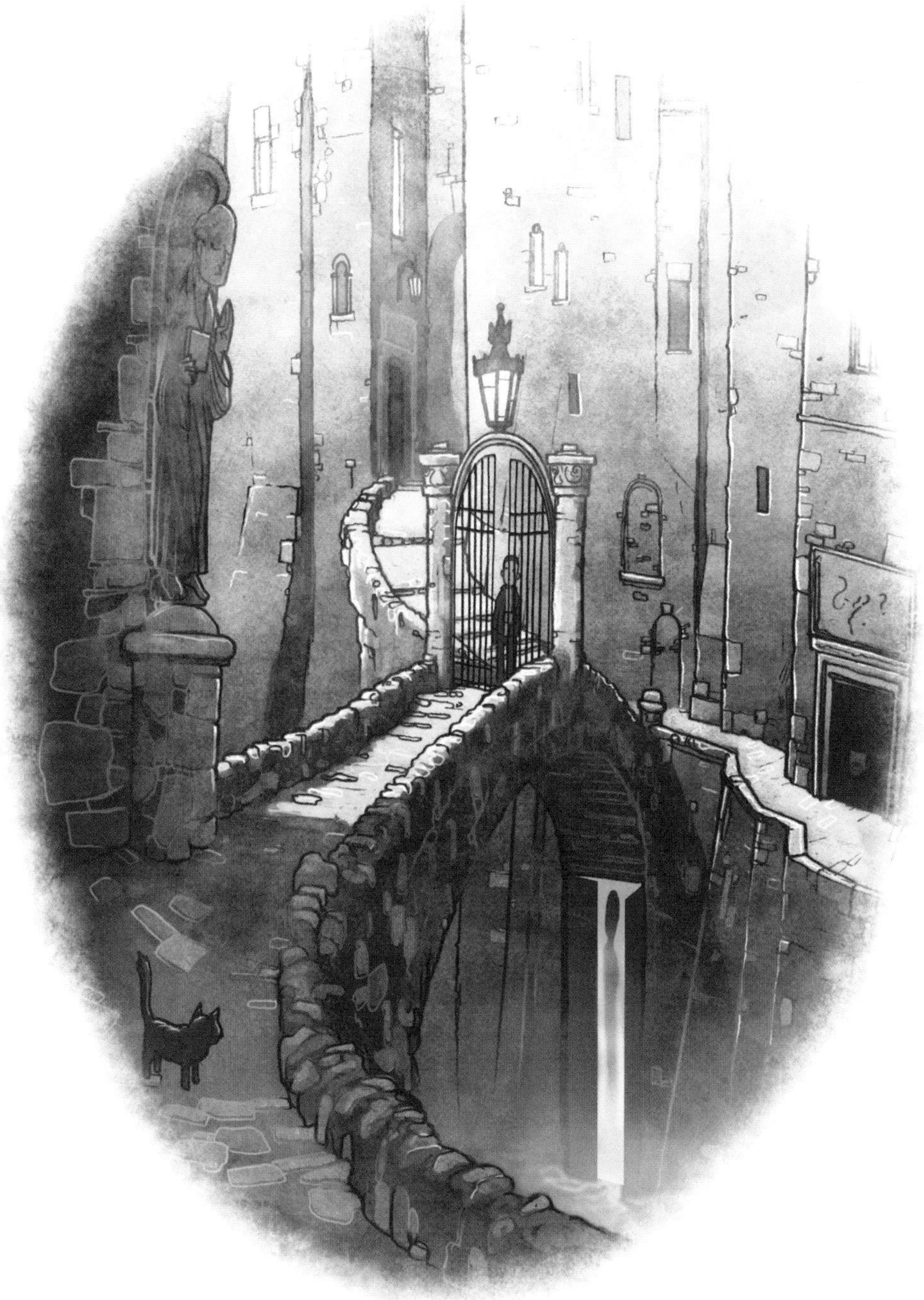

for many years the garden was left to go wild,
now it was overgrown and choked with weeds

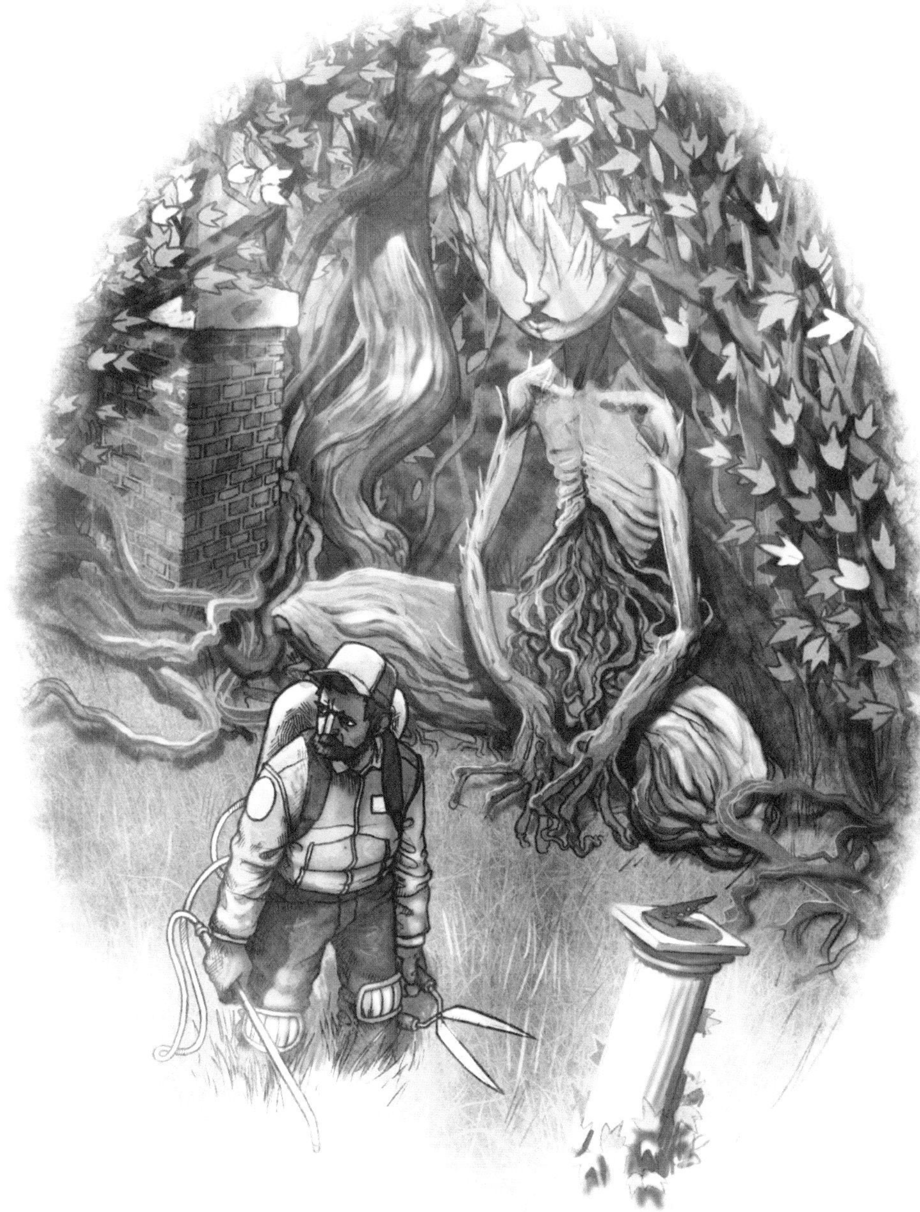

she lived at the top.
she never said or did anything
but he still hated sharing the lift with her

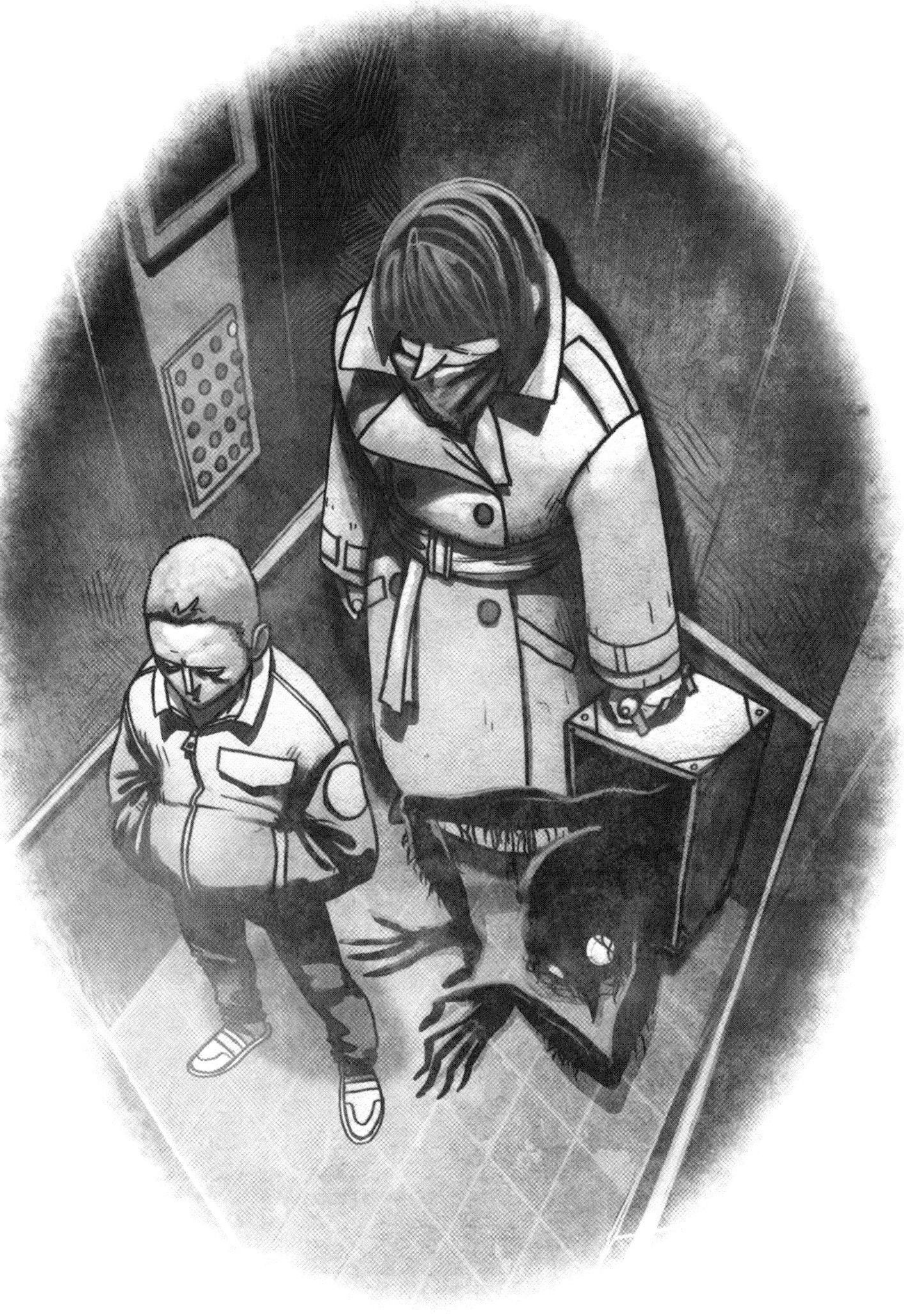

when she returned to her boat
it still sat alone on the tiny beach
but now she saw another set of tracks alongside her own

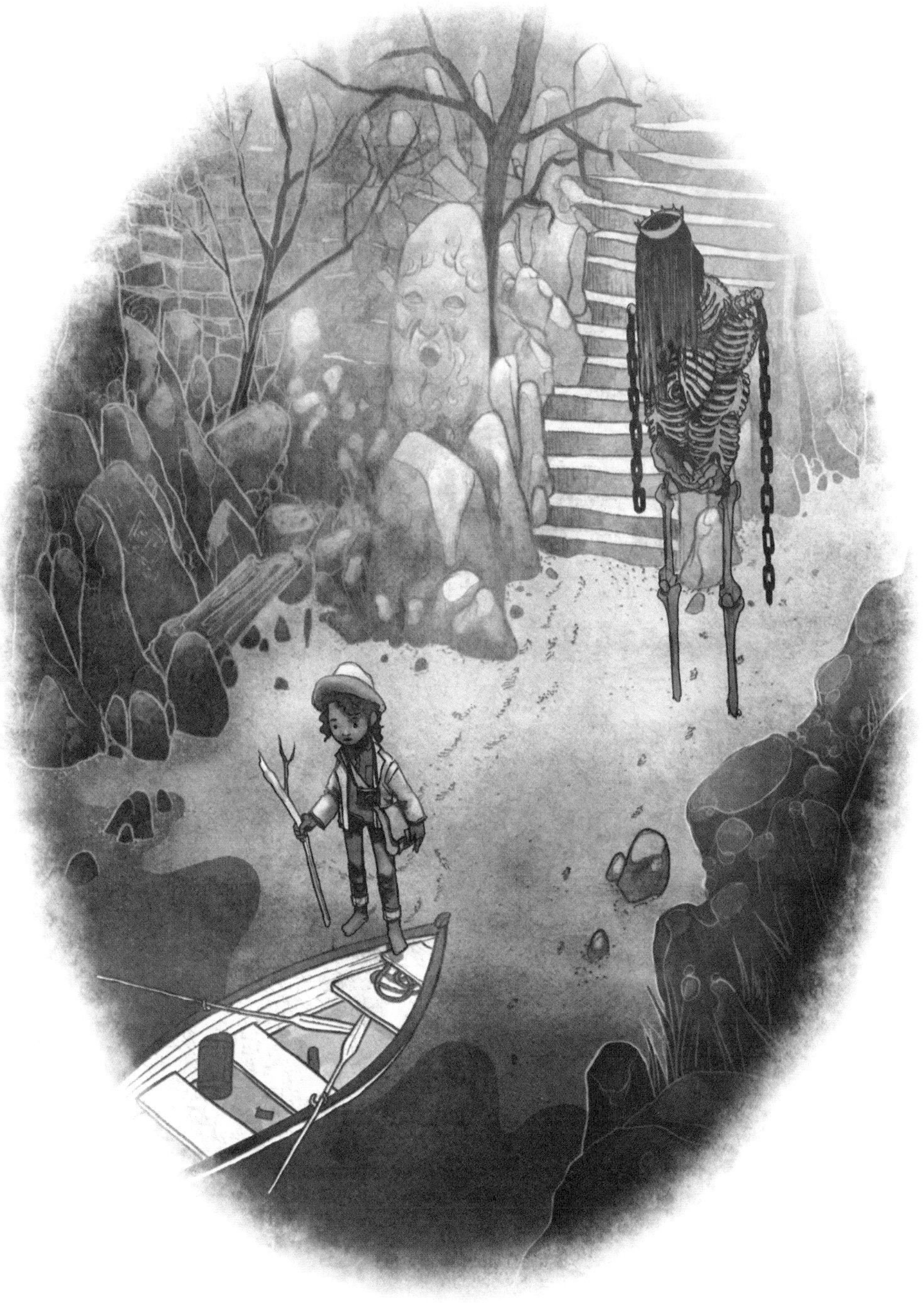

chattering and giggling,
bloody neighbours never shut up

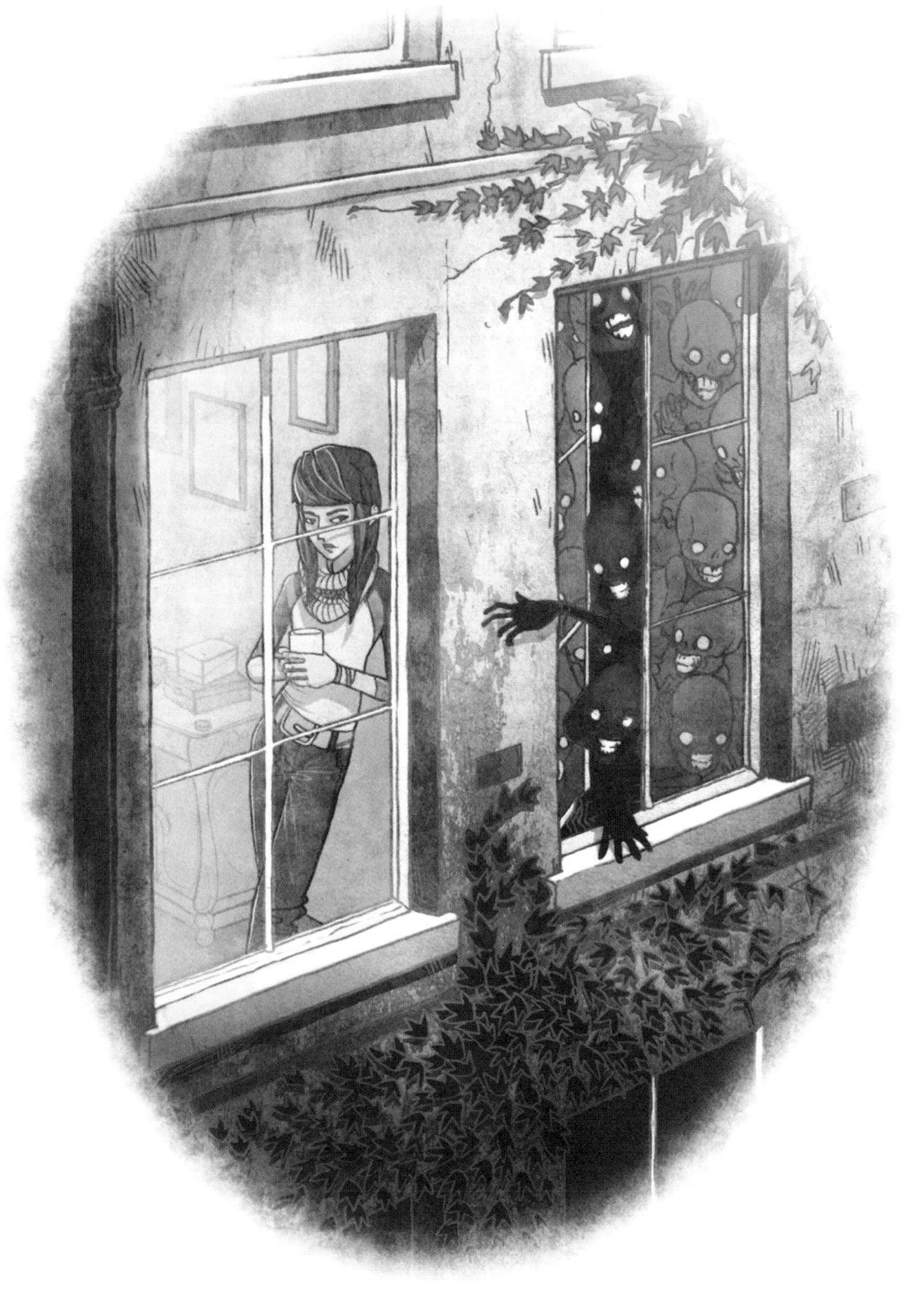

something was off.
either she couldn't follow directions
or the boy couldn't give them

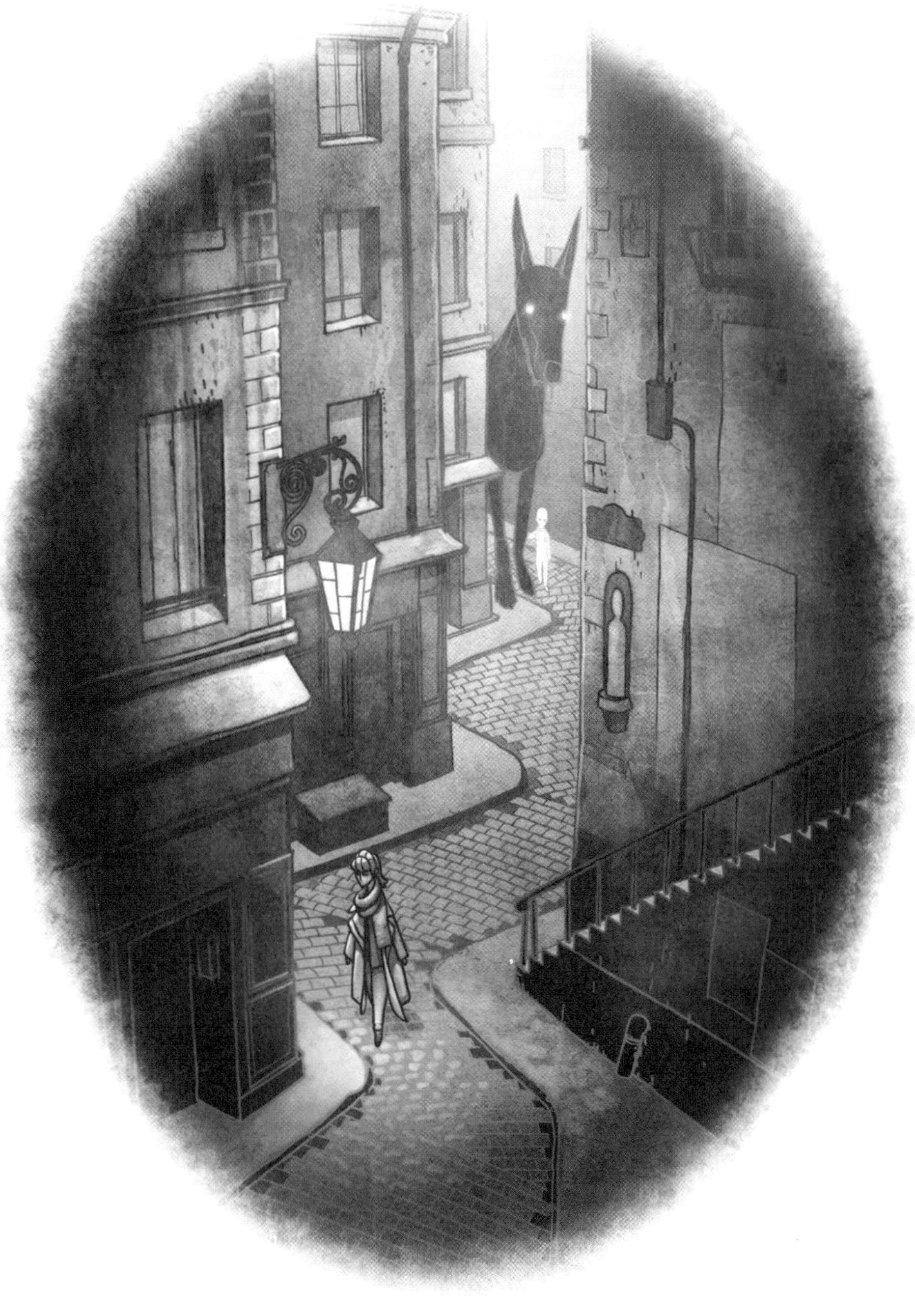

this crossroad was not on the map
and the many signposts were no help at all

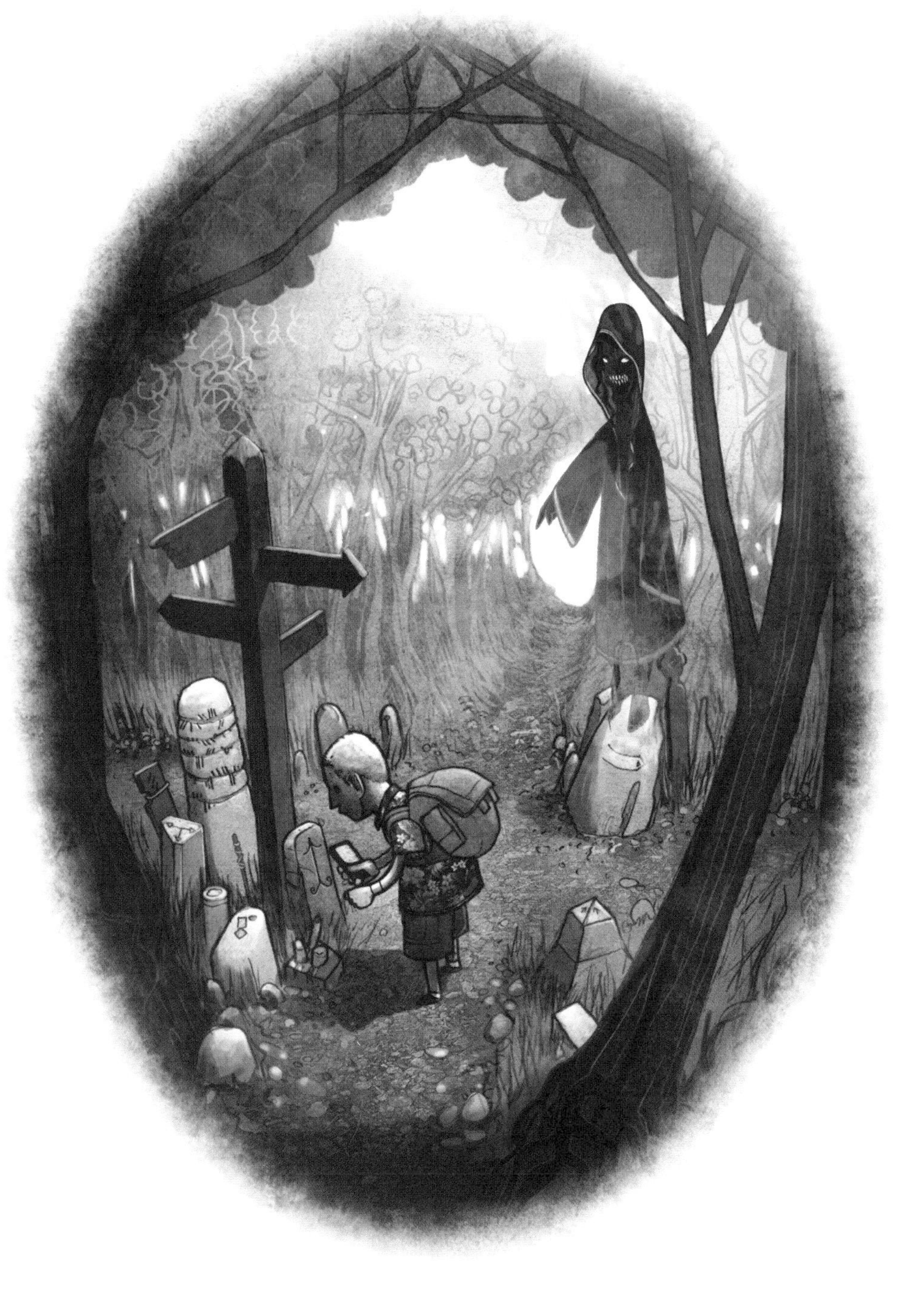

he loved to have the house to himself

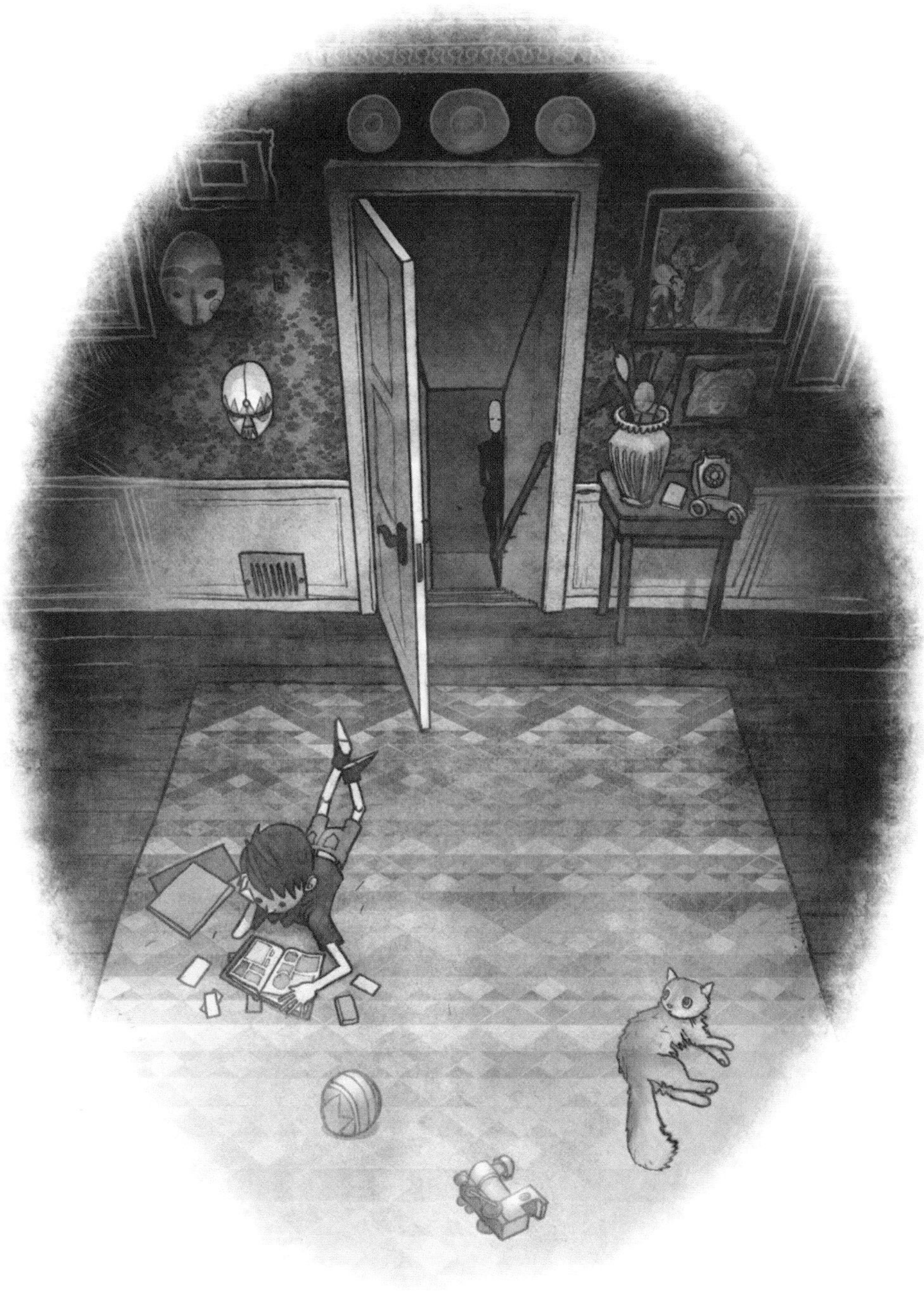

it only happened very rarely
but he hated when there was mail
to deliver to the whateley place

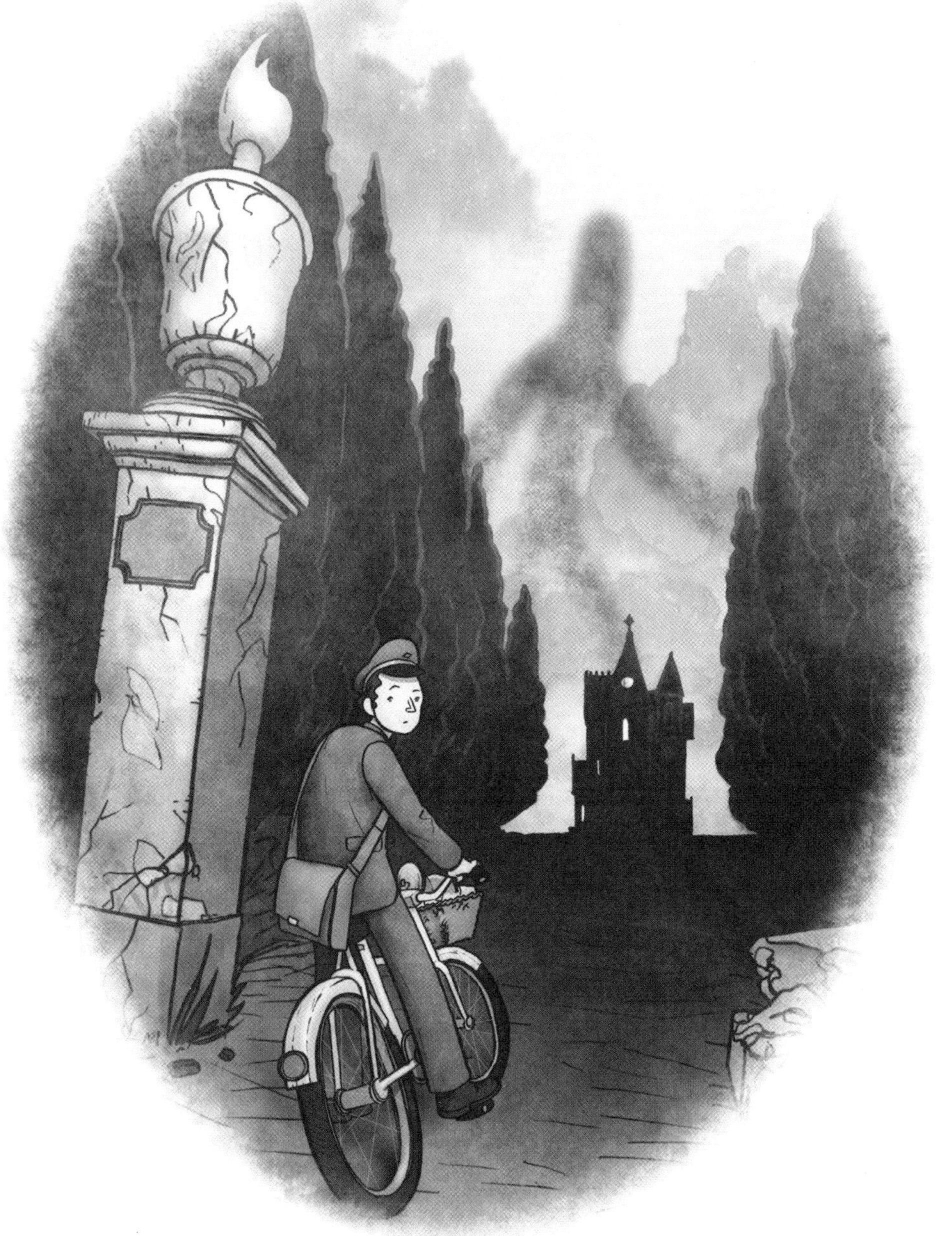

the garage was full and empty.
as he opened his car door he thought he heard a scream

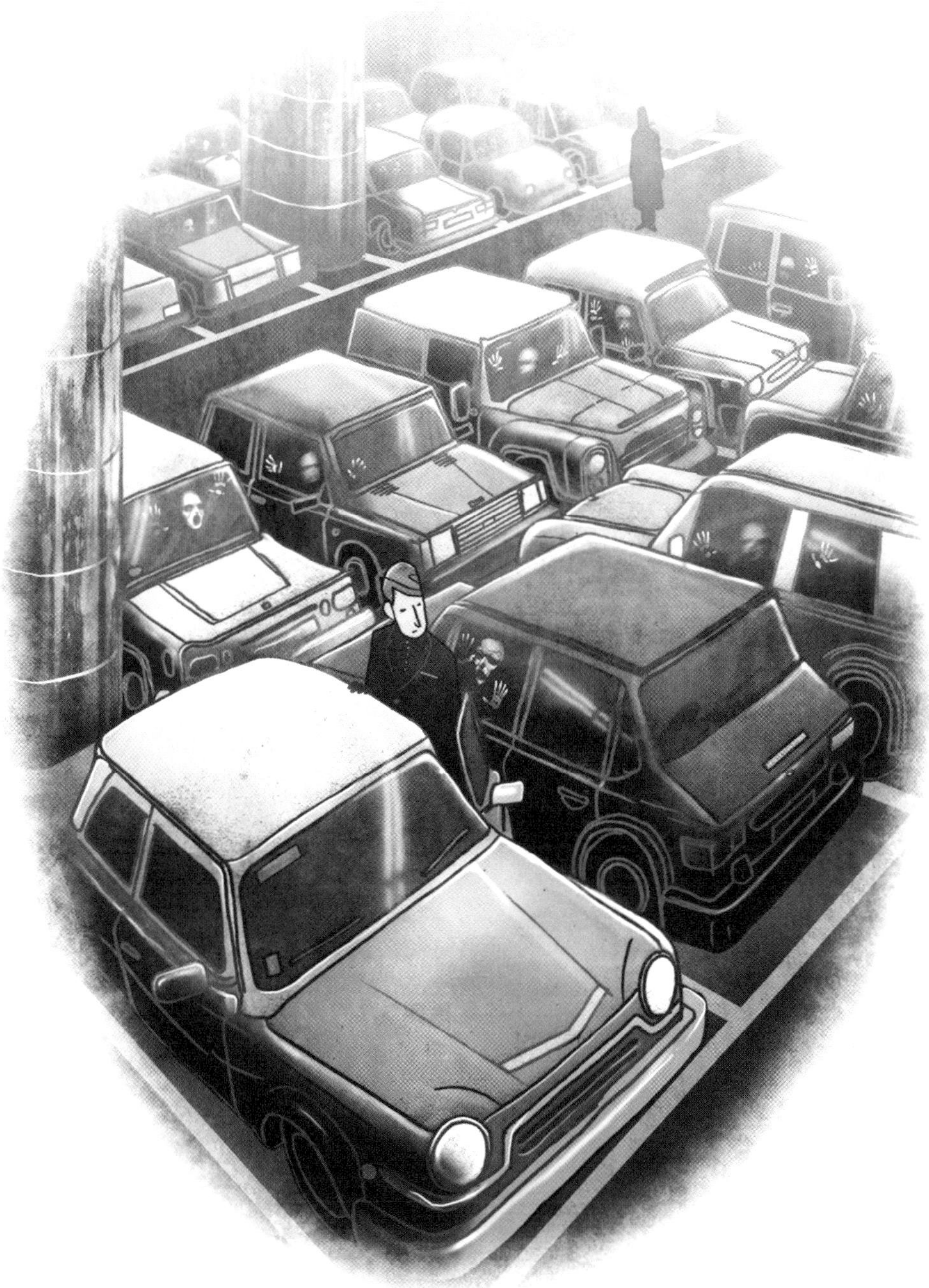

he asked and the echo answered

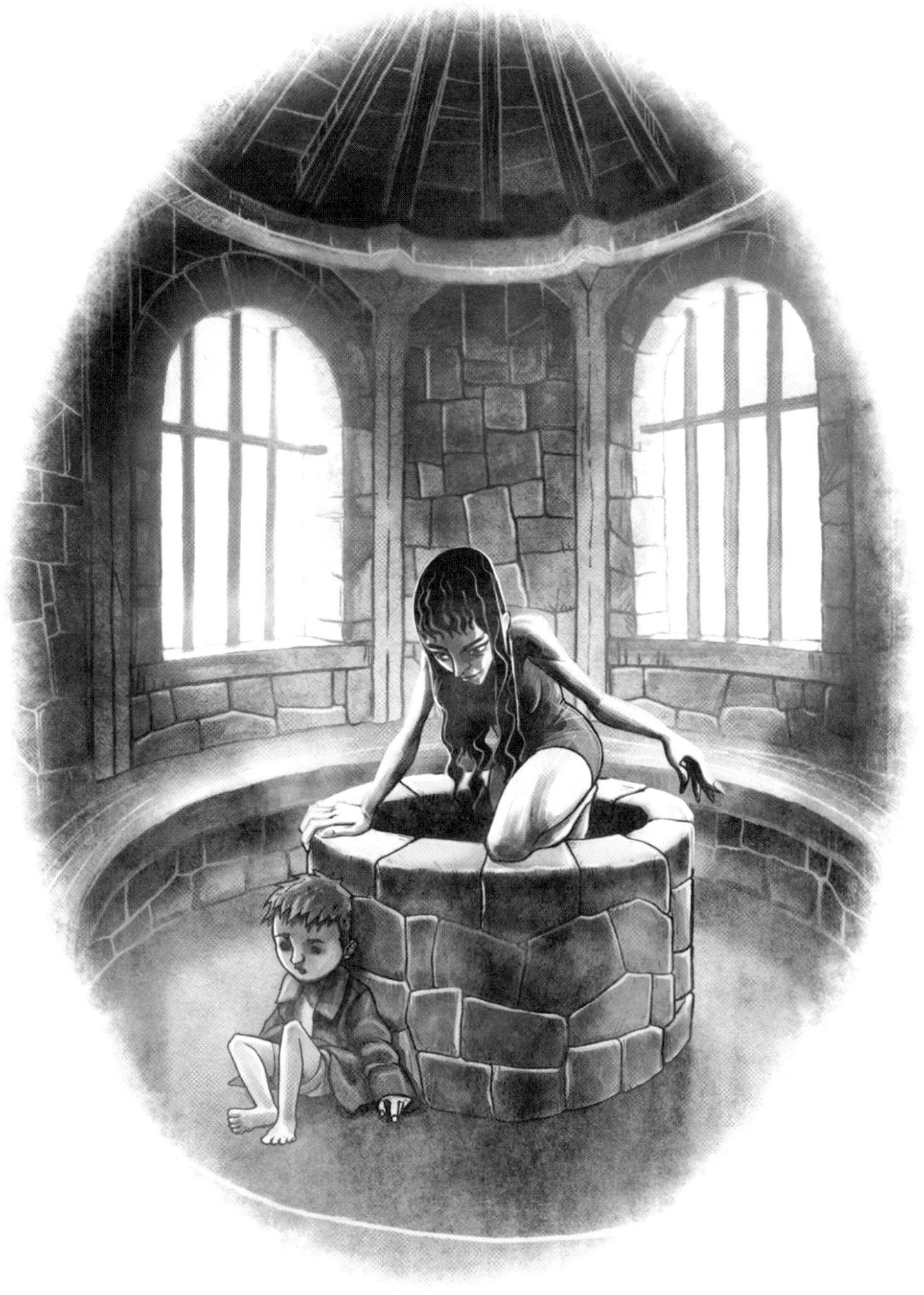

it was horrible, unimaginable.
someone had torn a page from one of the books

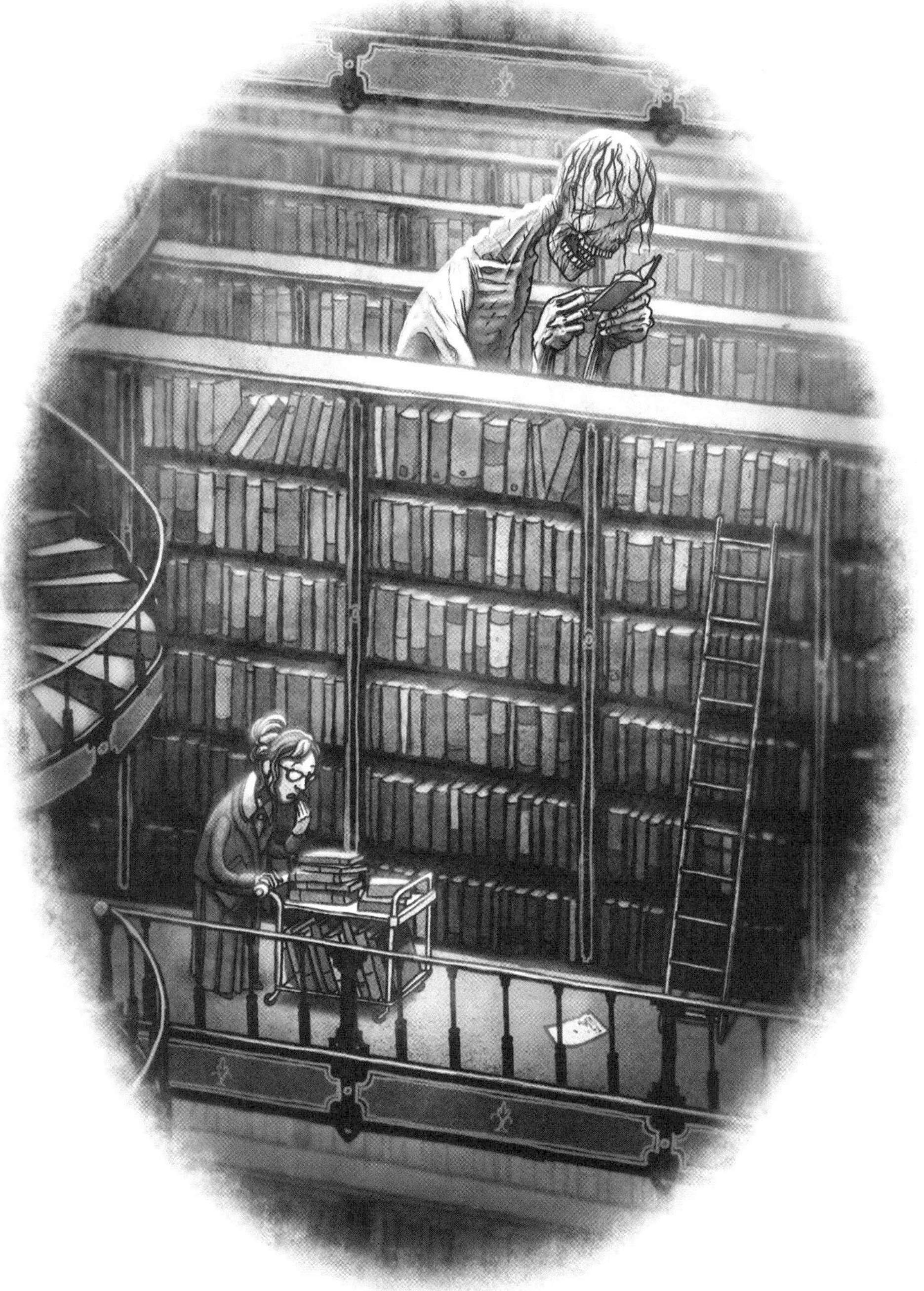

she didn't regret doing it,
she regretted getting caught.
now she was stuck in detention with the freaks

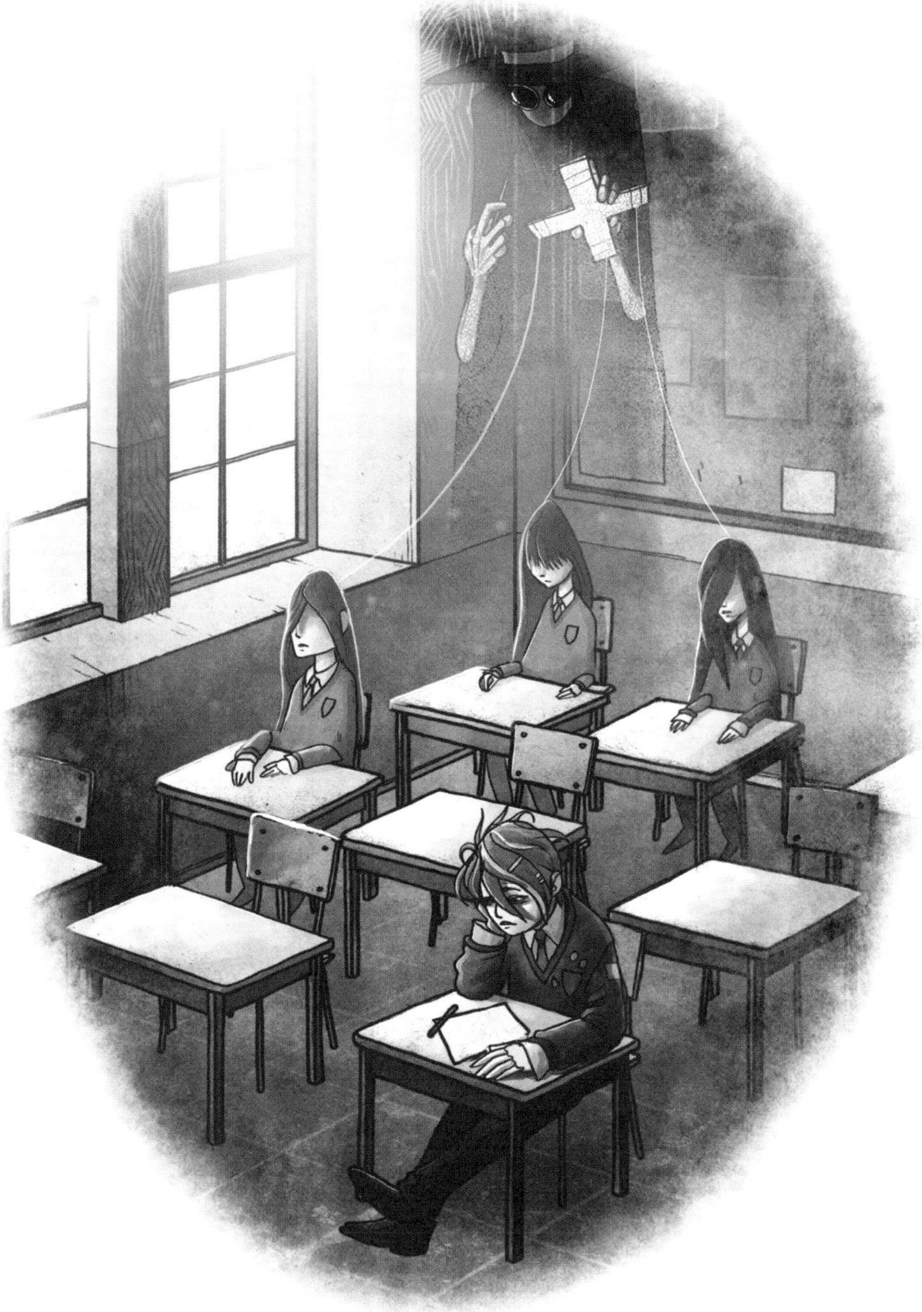

the ball had landed in the worst spot.
jenkin's garden was gross.
it was so wild you didn't know what was lurking in there

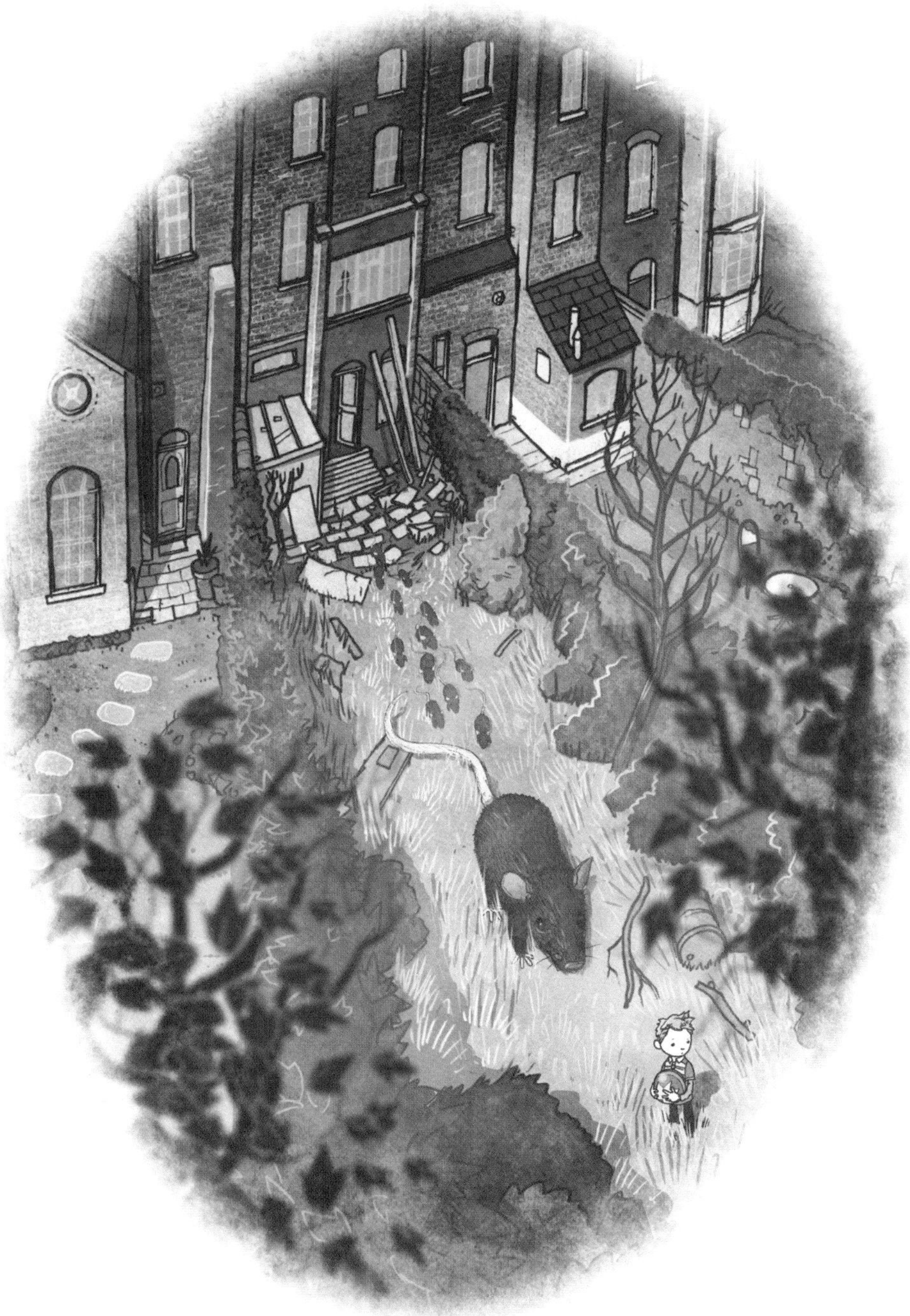

soon it would kick in,
he'd fall asleep,
then wake up with it all over and done with

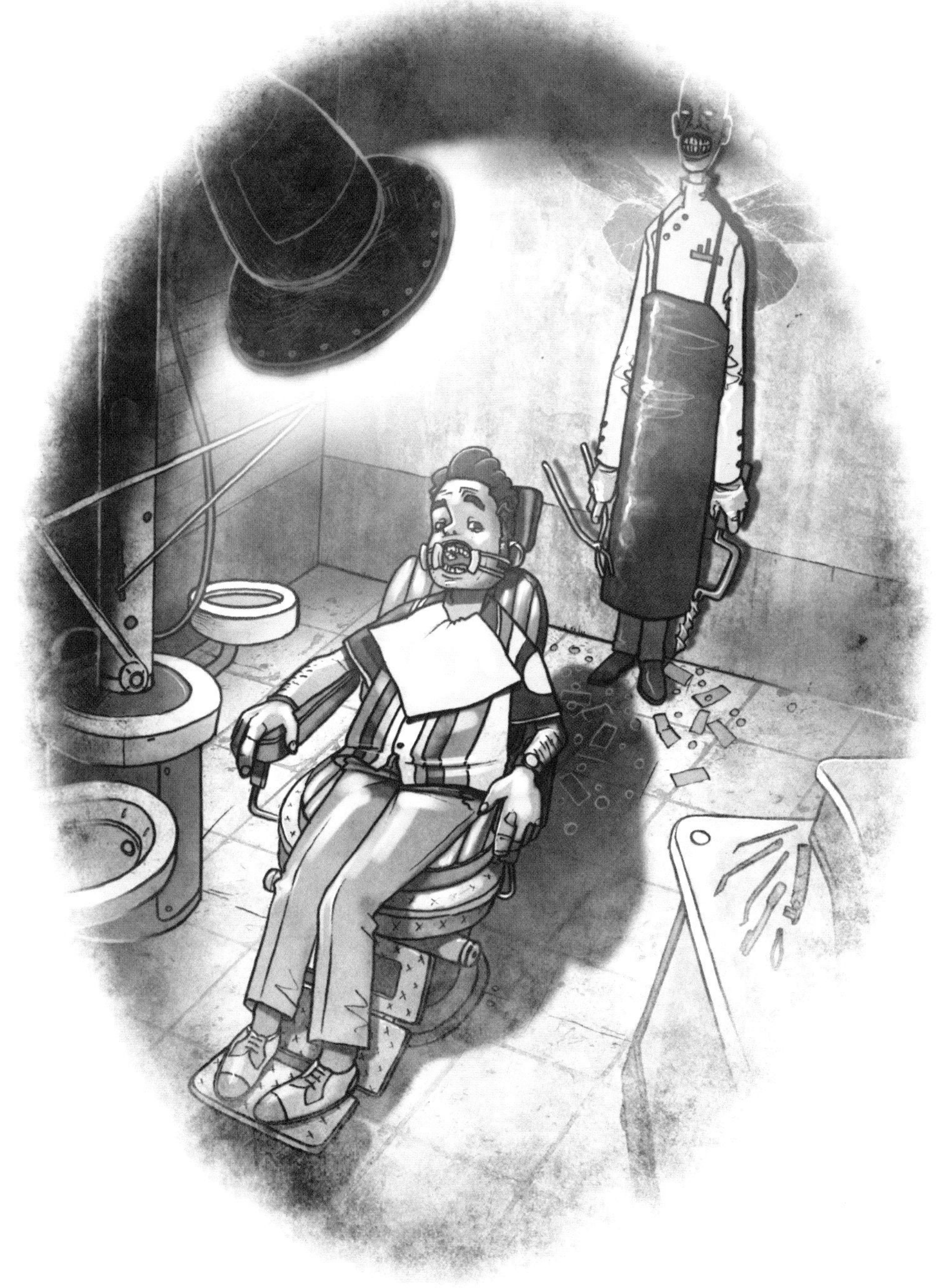

growing up sounded like a terrible idea.
if he changed completely could anyone be sure it was still him

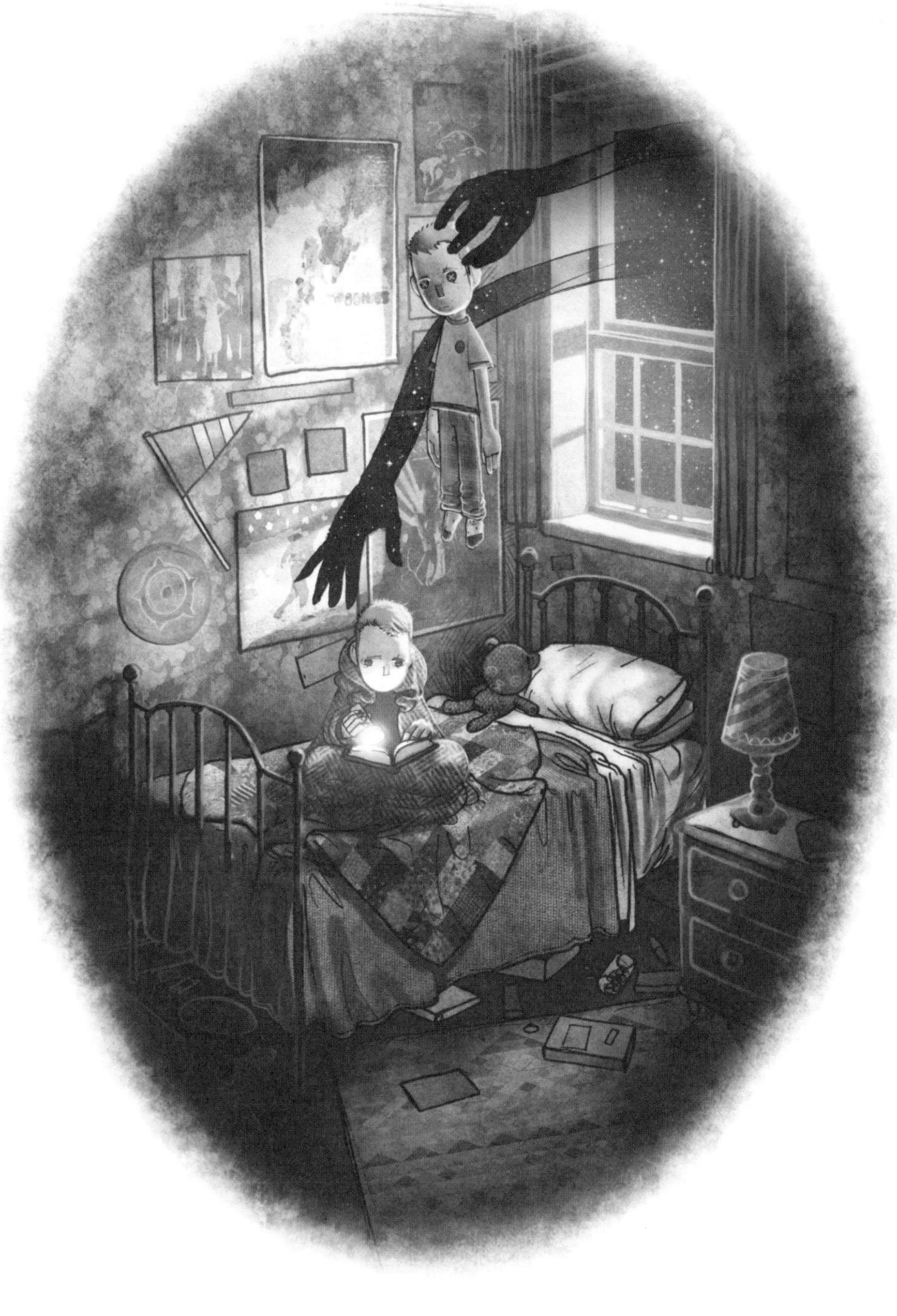

night callers were the worst.
this one just said over and over,
"hear my voice and I am with you"

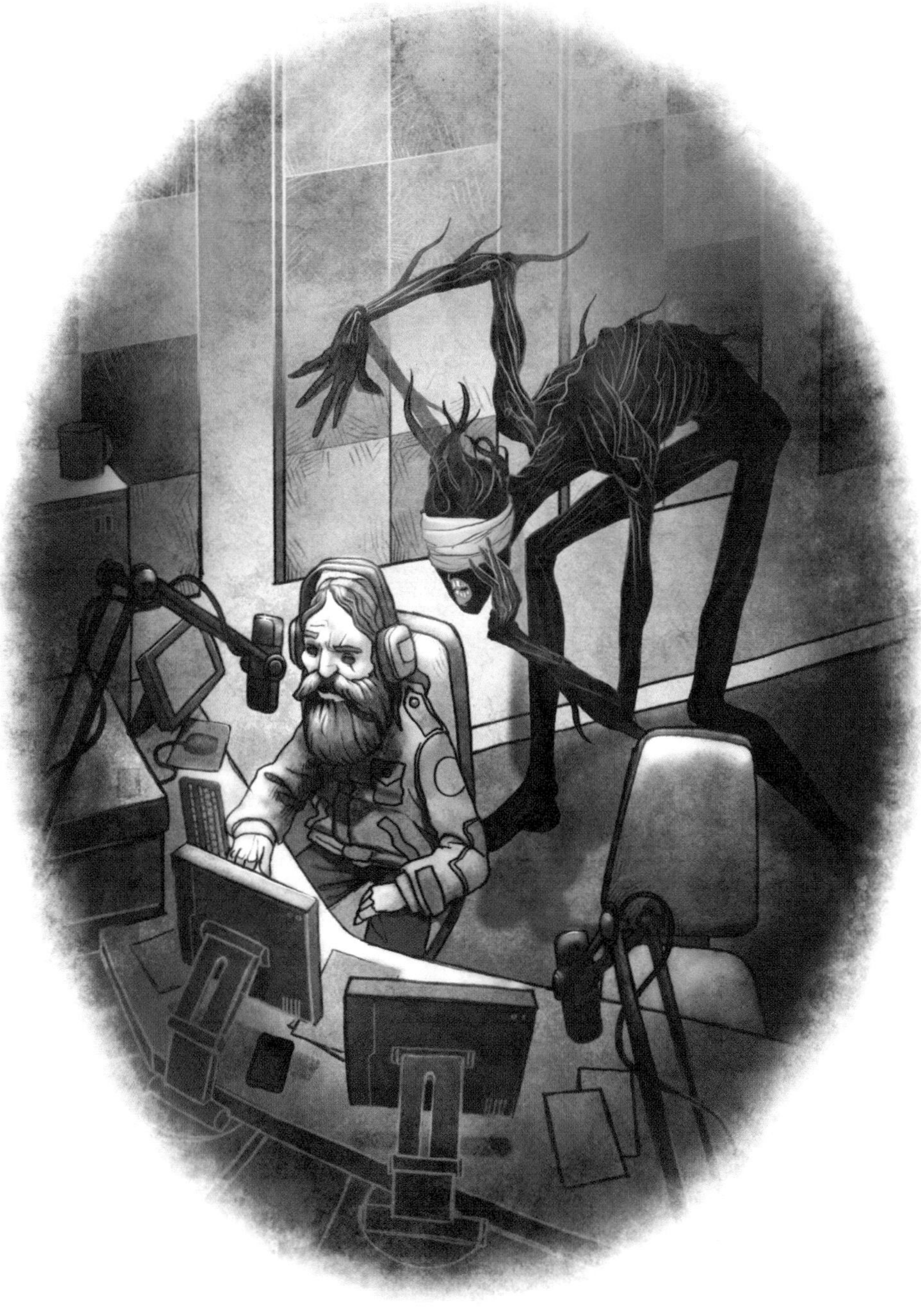

she began to feel foolish
for ever even considering that they would turn up

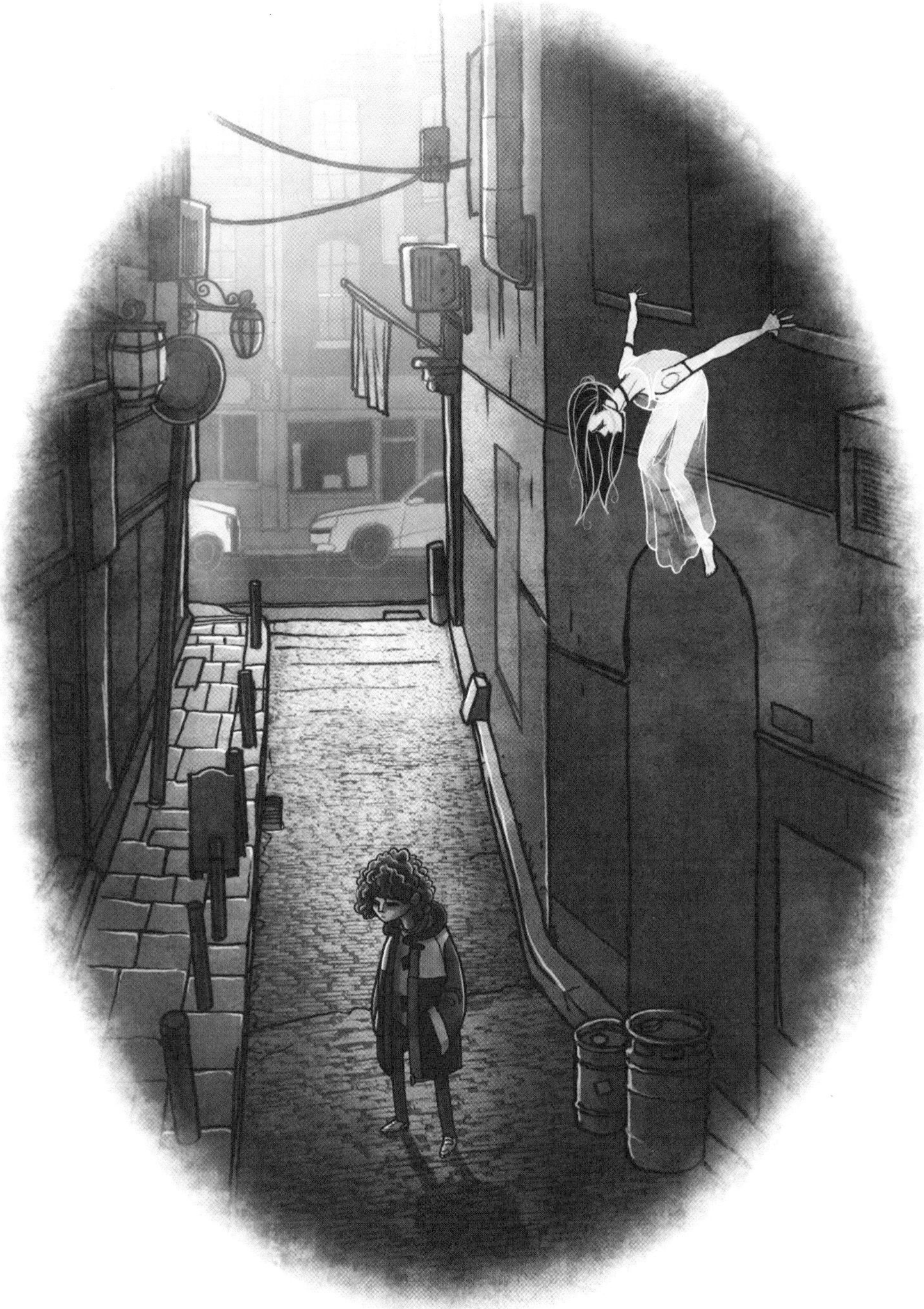

the pub was dead that night, not a soul about,
but then came a whisper...
"drink up"

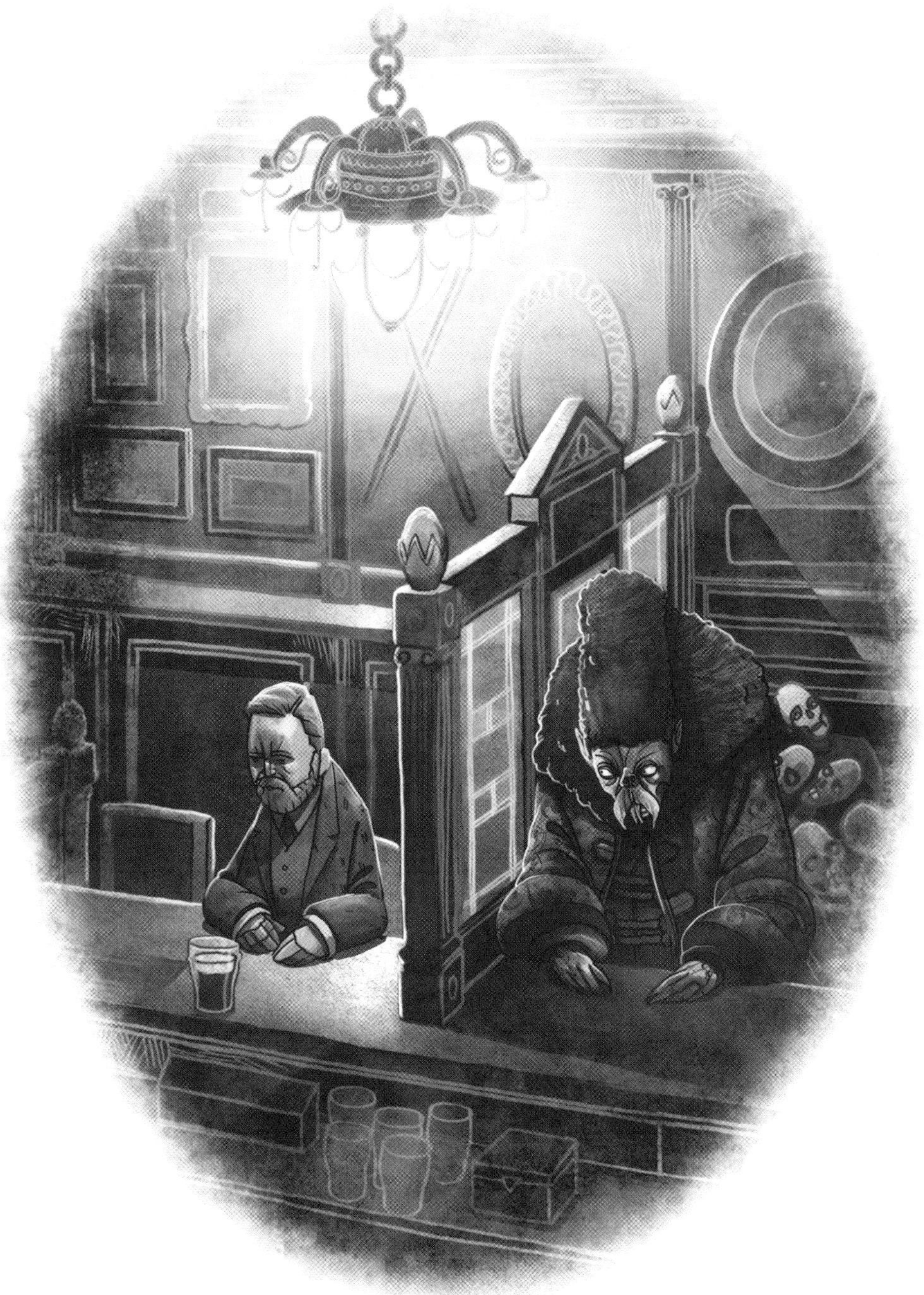

somewhere behind you

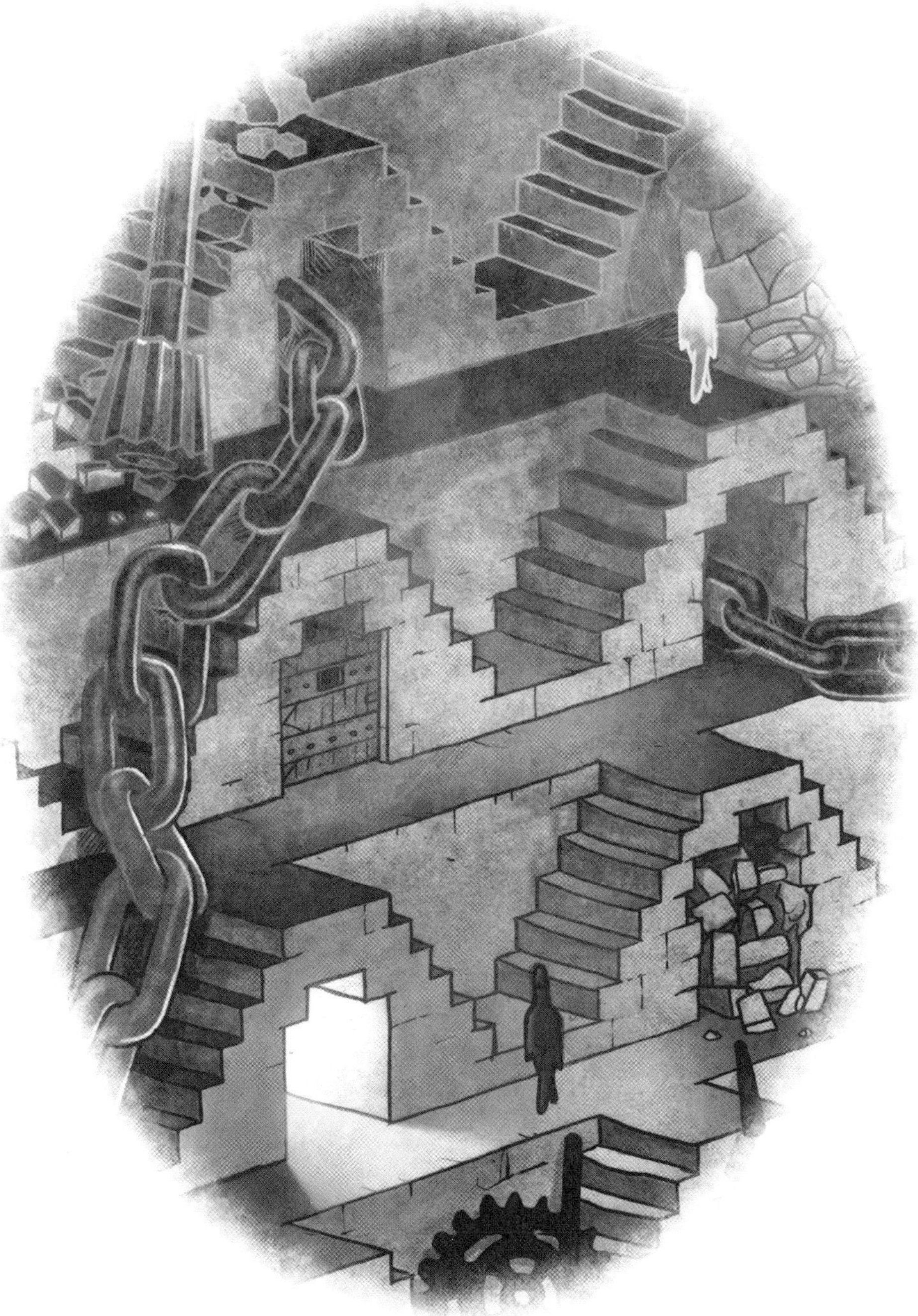

*she believed, if lit at the stroke of midnight,
the lantern would illuminate those
whose bodies were buried in the old cemetery*

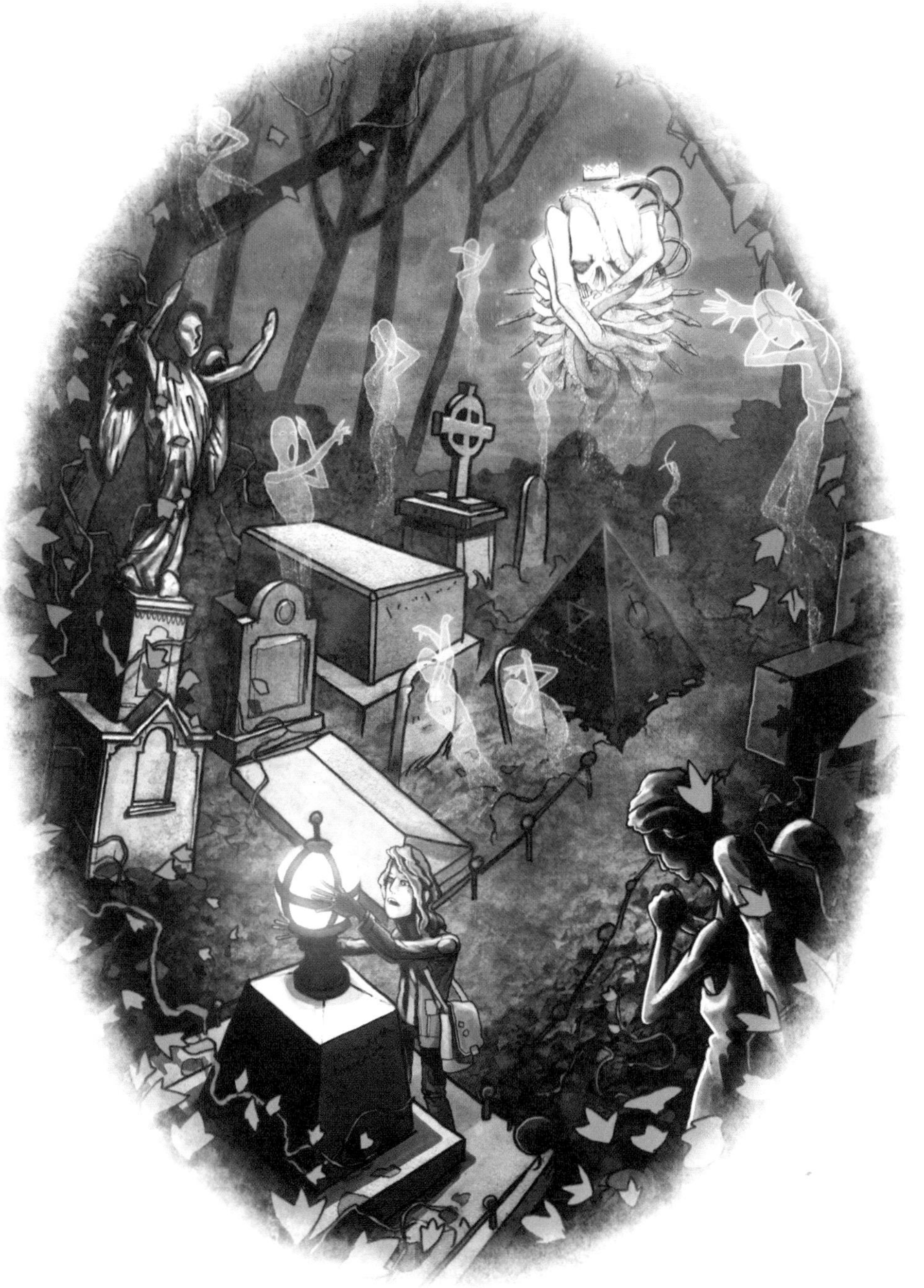

ever since he was a small boy
he had hated being underground.
he could not wait to get back out

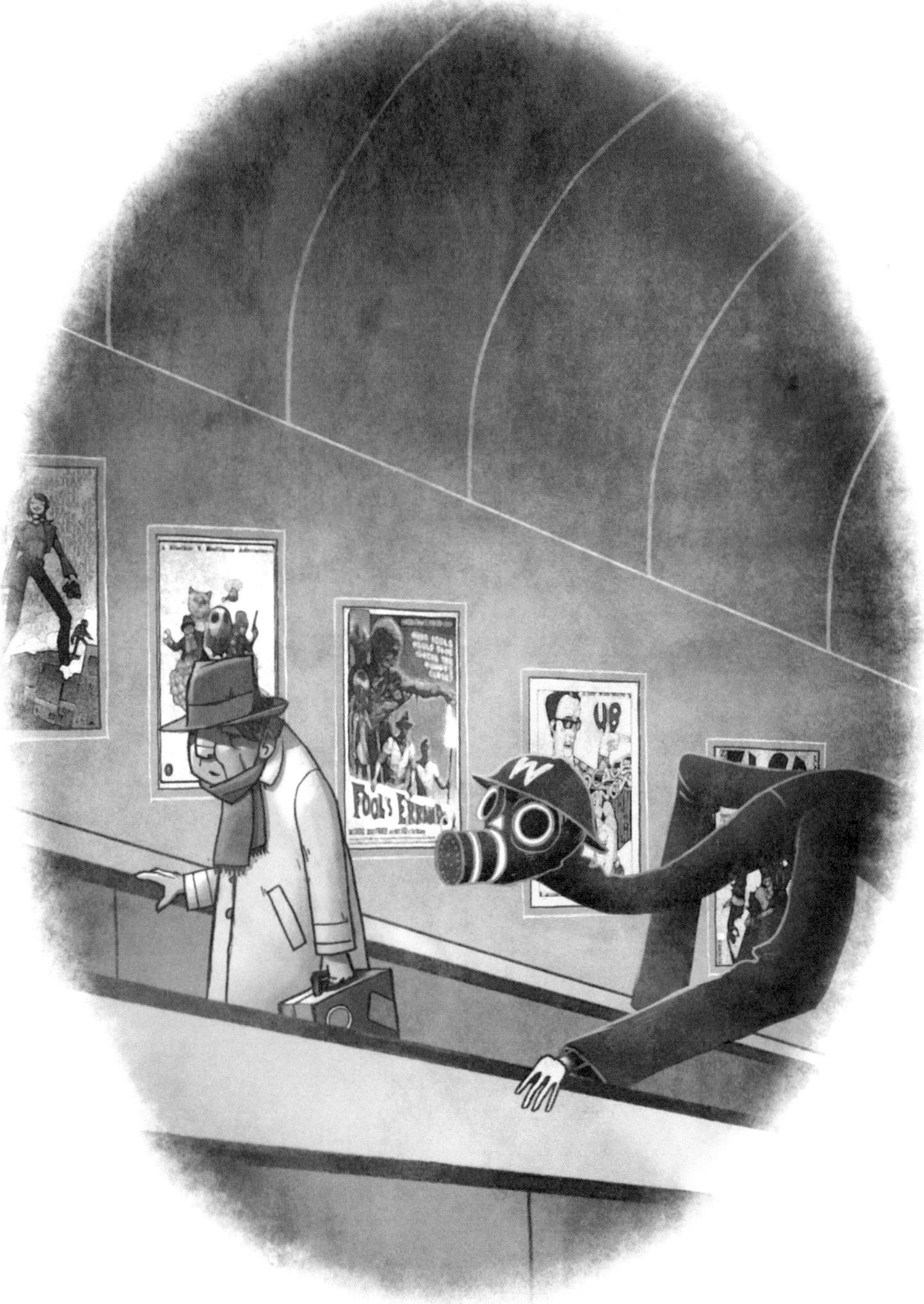
FOOL'S
UB
W

she didn't mind scary stories
but gram's story was too scary.
why was it set in her house?

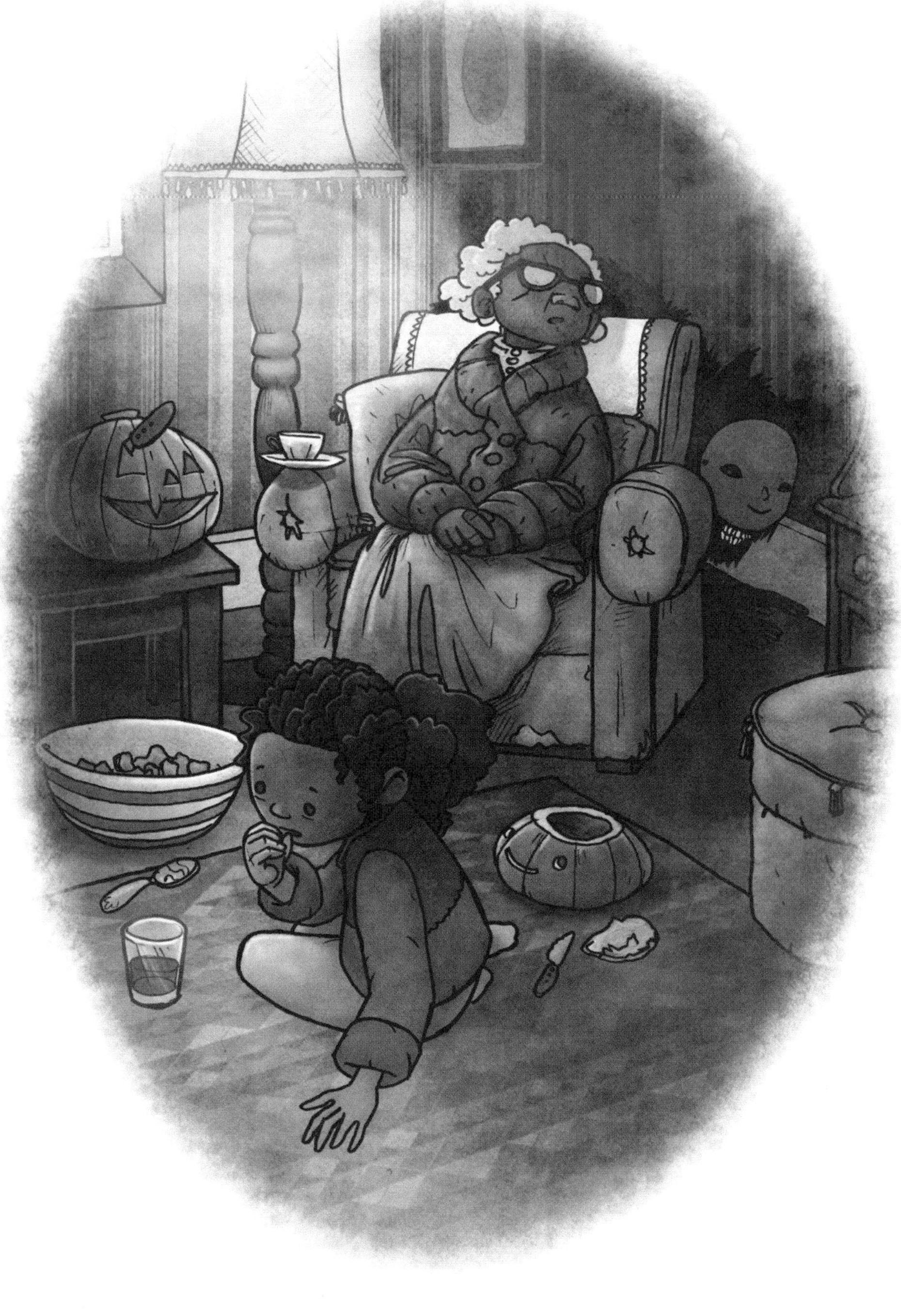

he knew it was selfish,
he didn't care.
he wanted all the treats to himself

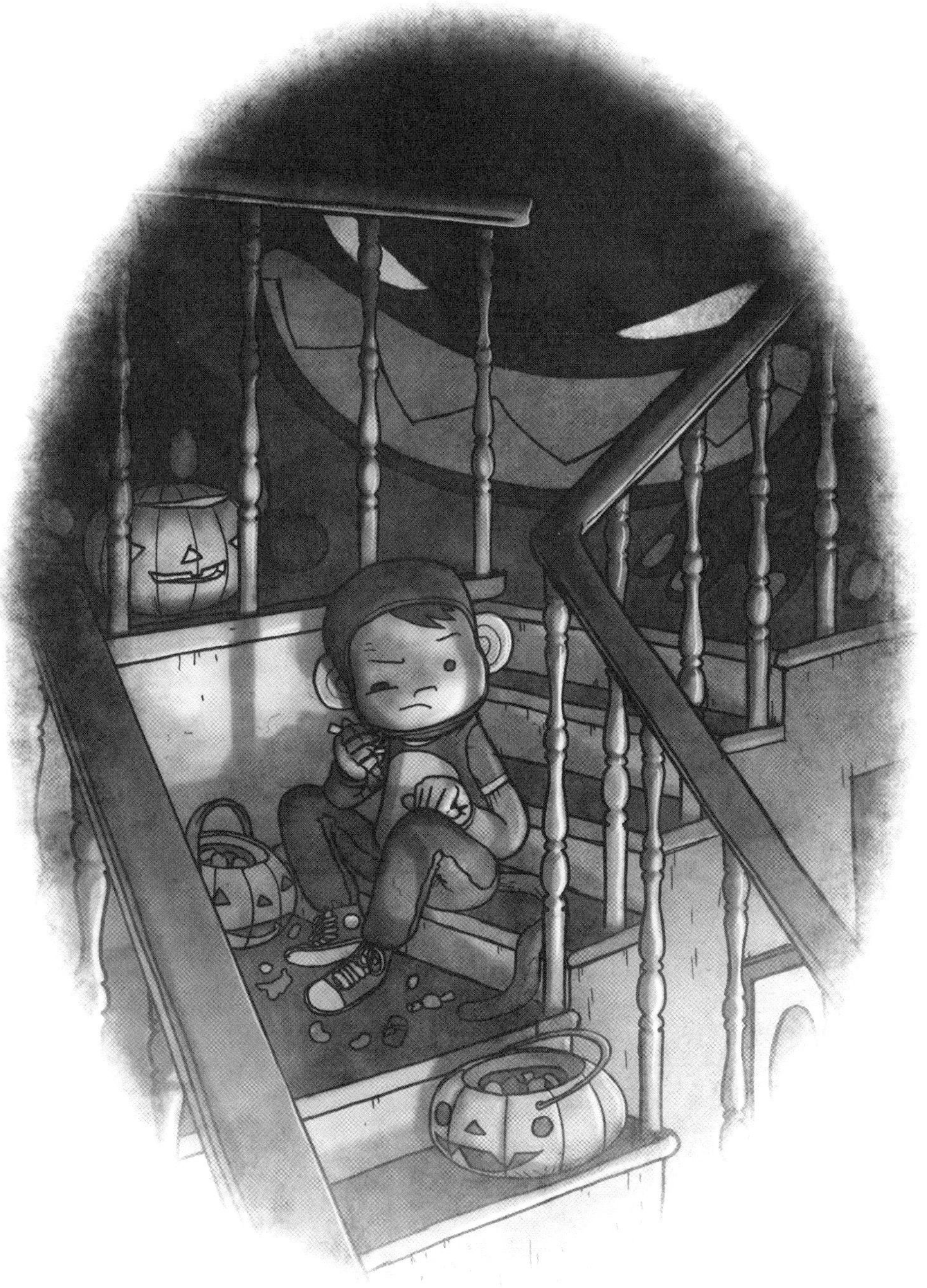

he was just glad to have an excuse to still dress up,
even if it was minding his sister
and the neighbour's kids

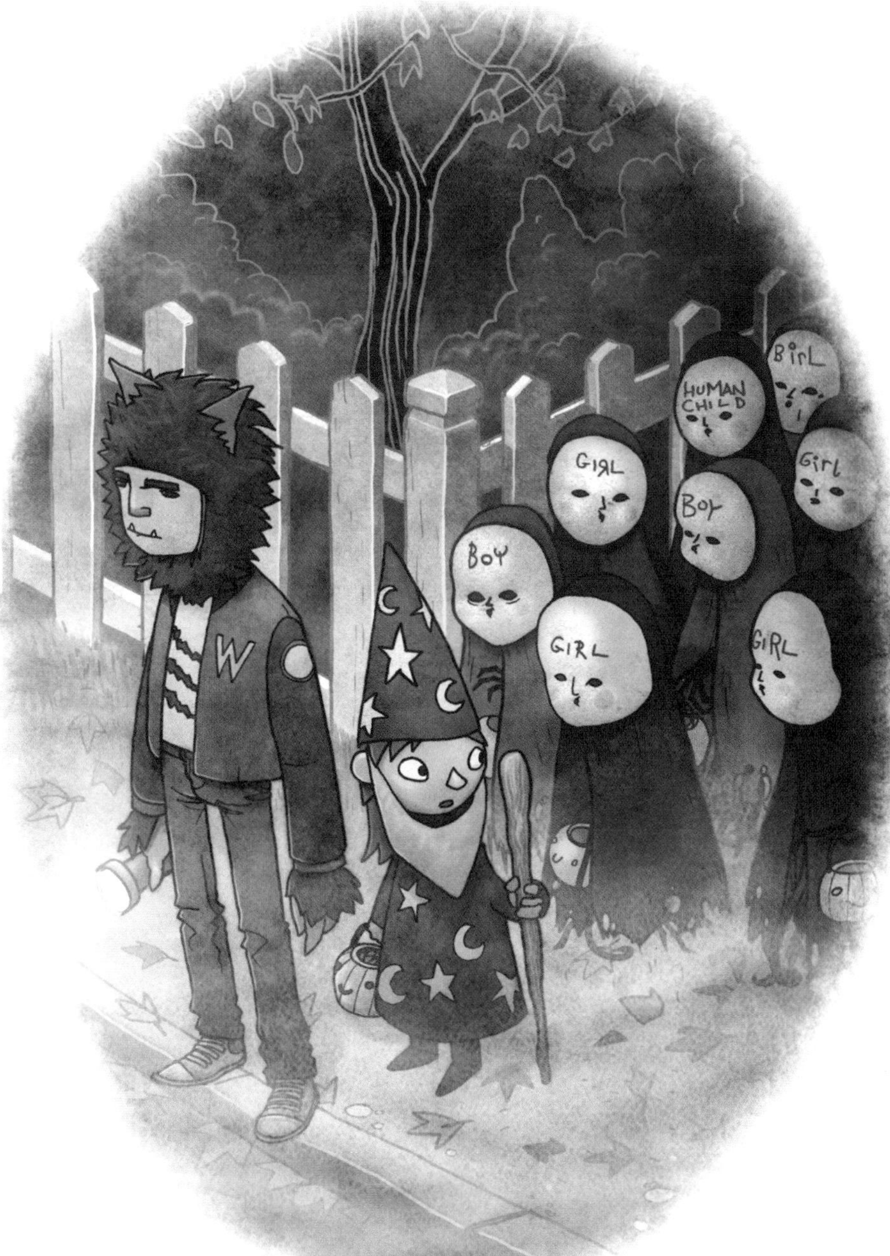
W
BirL
HUMAN CHILD
GIRL
Girl
BOY
BOY
GIRL
GIRL

...meow?

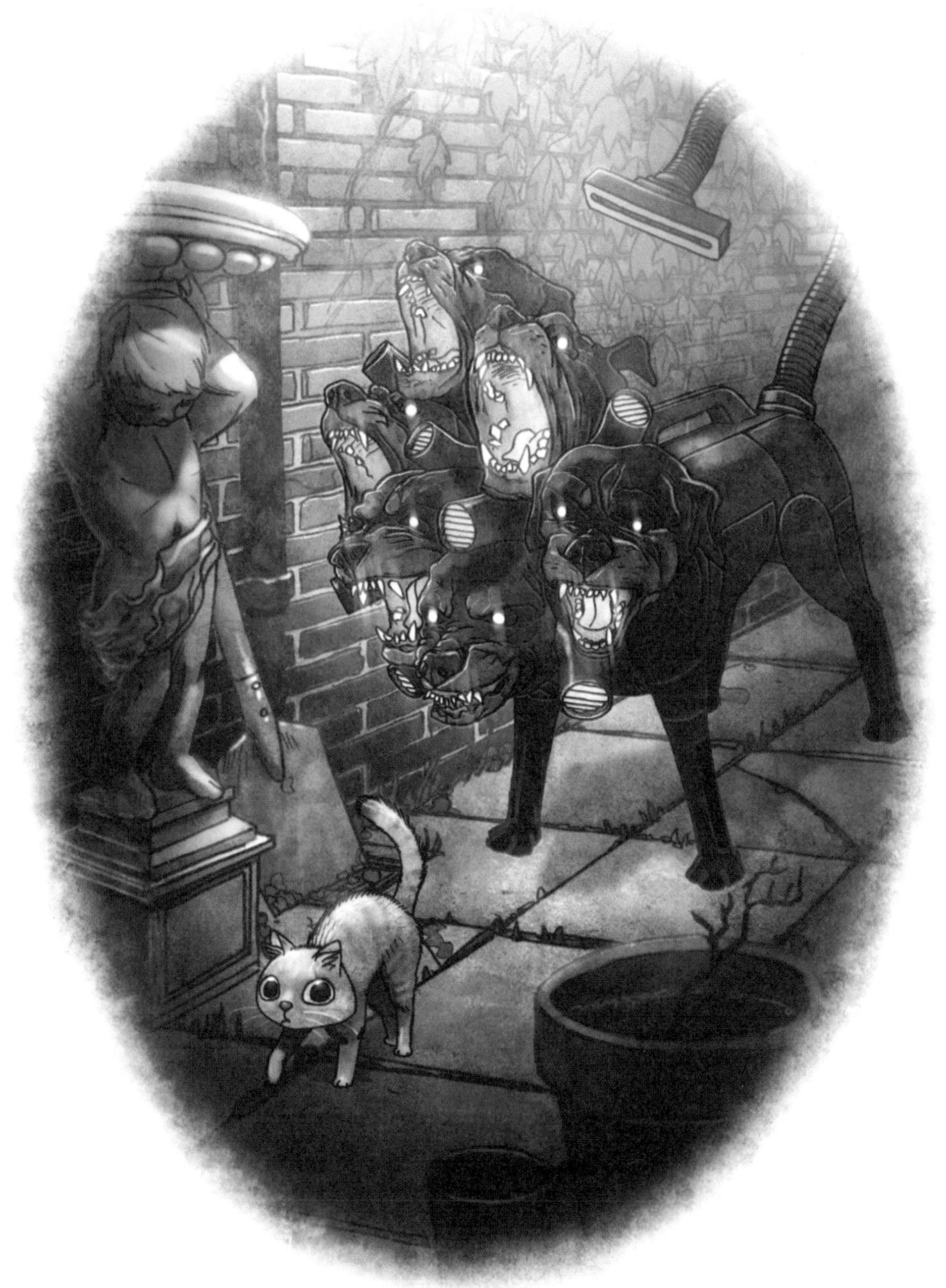

*i just knew you'd look great
sitting on my dashboard lil' fella*

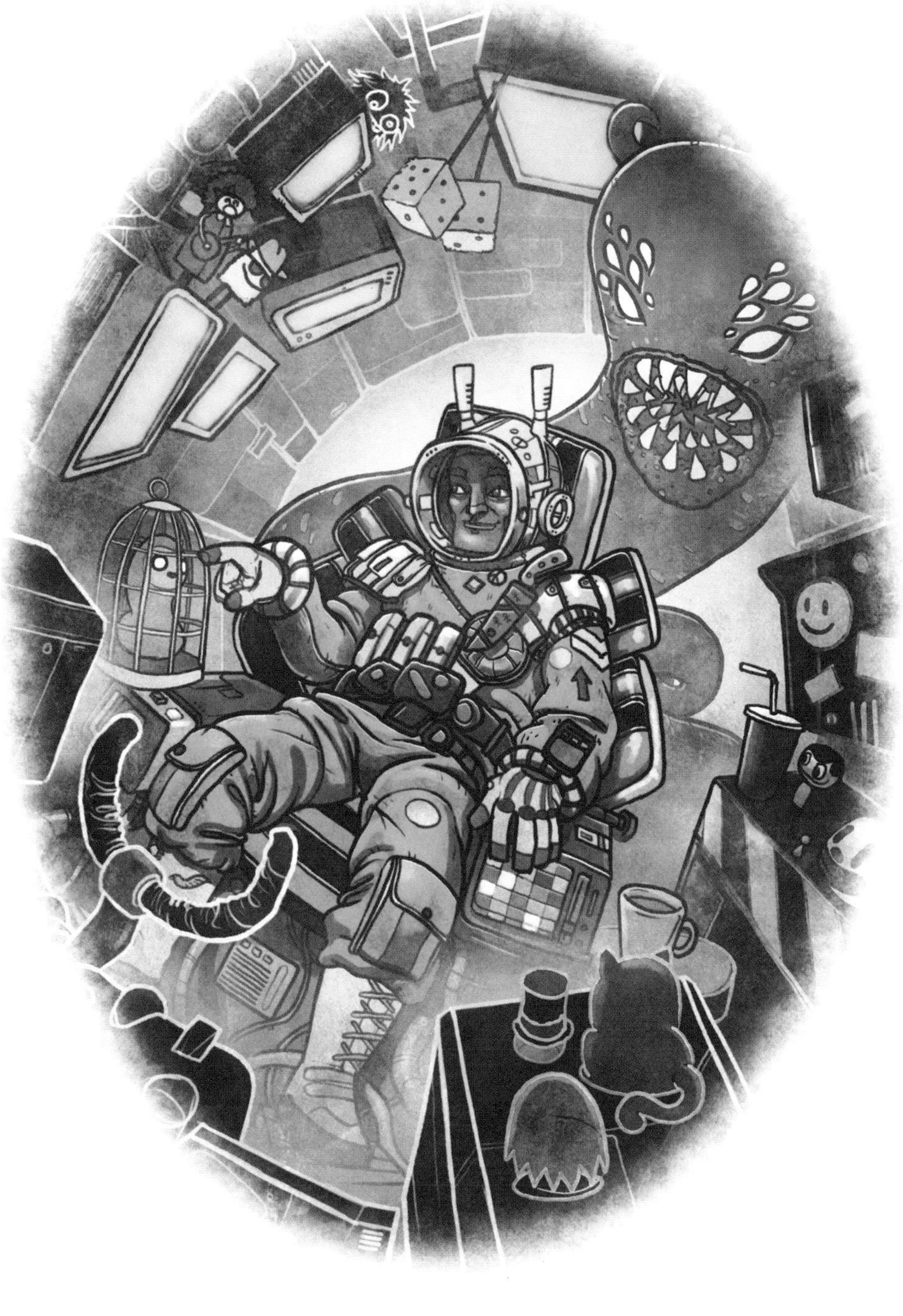

he knew it was out there.
hiding in the trees

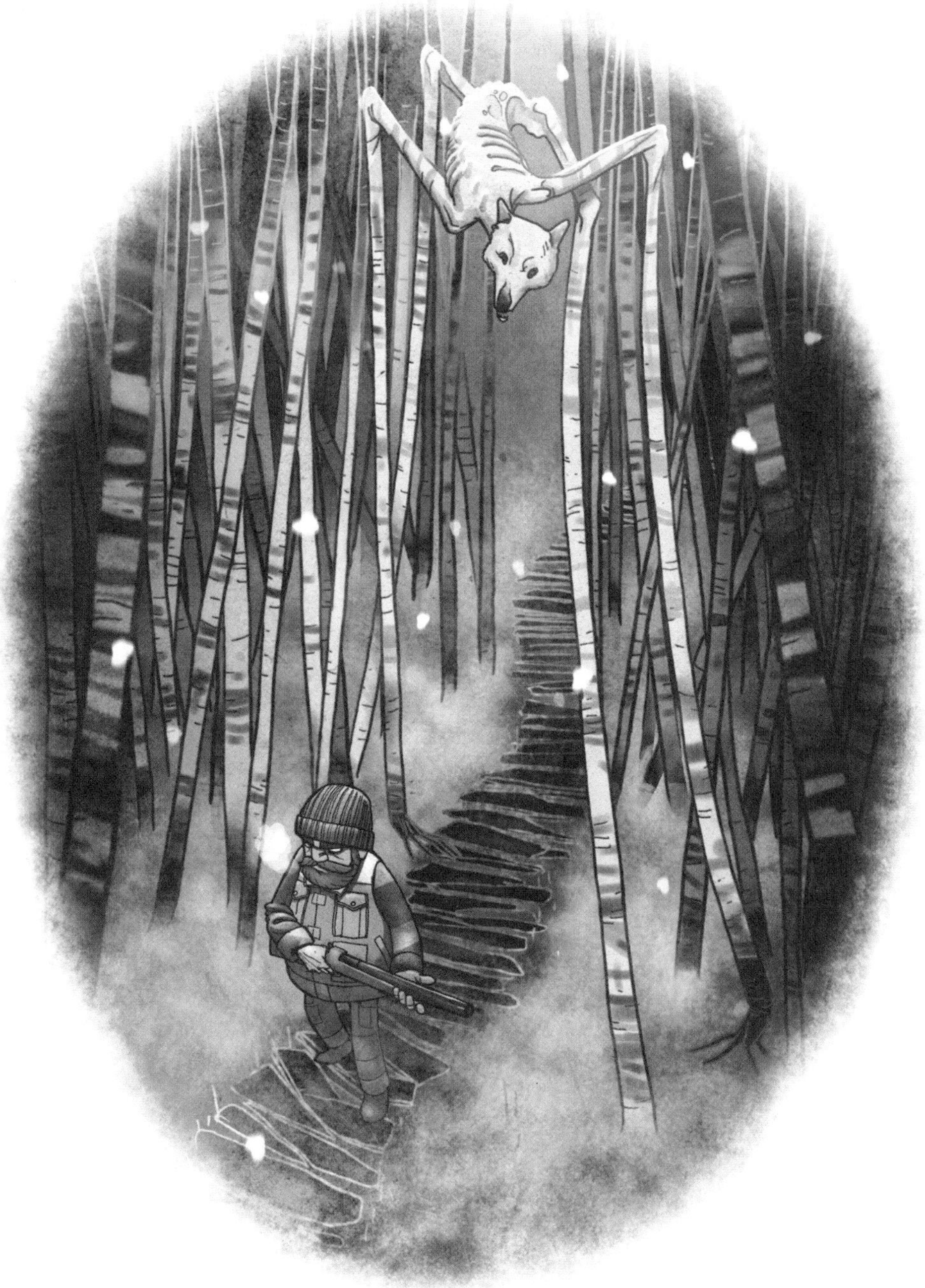

Thanks

*Rob Mayor, Martina Hawkins, Lorraine Nolan,
Sharna Rothwell, Kate Neary, Marko Kudjerski,
Sebastian Kristinsson, Steven Saus, Jen Tracy,
Heath Wolfeld, Natalie Simpson, Avery Beckett,
Benjamin Russell, Amy (Other Amy), Ryan Cagle,
Darren Fox, Michael Hearle, Quin Gorsuch,
Julie O'Donnell, Catherine Escobar, Bear Weiter,
Bruce Cordell, Sean K Reynolds, Jack E. Chambers,
Kira Butler, Jason Frank, David C. Escobar,
Linnea Seidegard, Chris Krovatin, Sean Zoltek,
Alexander Stiehl, Ali Lens Auld, Georg Moog,
Thomas DiPaolo, Kristen's Cavern stickers,
Sarah McCarthy, Alejandro Brugues,
Kayla Wood, David M, Nora Sawyer, Billy,
Tom B, Thomas Pluck, Lunafaaye, Turtlesong,
Squeek, Nina Bouvier, Heather M, Sam Kroll,*

*Chris Ryall, Justin Eisinger, Alonzo Simon
Joe Hill*

Kate & Grumpuss